C000319175

Mills & Boon Classics

A chance to read and collect some of the best-loved novels from Mills & Boon—the world's largest publisher of romantic fiction.

Every month, four titles by favourite Mills & Boon authors will be re-published in the *Classics* series.

A list of other titles in the *Classics* series can be found at the end of this book.

Anne Mather

DARK MOONLESS NIGHT

MILLS & BOON LIMITED
LONDON · TORONTO

First published 1974
Australian copyright 1980
Philippine copyright 1980
This edition 1980

© Anne Mather 1974

ISBN 0 263 73445 5

Set in 10/12 pt. Linotype Plantin

Made and printed in Great Britain by
Richard Clay (The Chaucer Press) Ltd,
Bungay, Suffolk

CHAPTER ONE

THE Boeing had landed in the early hours of the morning, local time, and there had been little to see but the lights of the airport; which, as far as Caroline could remember, had been much the same as any other airport she had visited, except of course that all the personnel were black. It had been cold, too, much colder than one would have imagined a place to be that was within a couple of hundred miles of the Equator. There had been the usual landing procedure, the usual delays with passport control and Customs, but then they had been free to take the company car to the hotel.

David and Miranda had been fractious, which hadn't really been surprising. Any young child would be fractious at having to be wakened from a sound sleep to face a series of irritating airport formalities, and even Elizabeth had been inclined to moan a little. It had been left to Caroline to marshall their suitcases for the black chauffeur and cope with two small pairs of clinging hands, both of which demanded her undivided attention.

At last they had all been able to pile into the back of the opulent limousine sent by Freelong Copper Incorporated to meet the wife and family of one of its minor executives. They had been driven along a smooth, tarmacked highway to Ashenghi, Tsaba's capital, and installed in a luxurious hotel in the very heart of the city. Then the chauffeur had departed leaving them to explore the comfortable suite of rooms which had been put at their disposal.

Elizabeth had said it had all been too much, much too much, and she had pleaded exhaustion and a raging headache before taking herself off to seek the cool sheets of her bed. Consequently, it was Caroline who gave the children their brief but thorough wash, helped them into their pyjamas, and tucked them up in the twin beds in the room adjoining her own. And it had been Caroline who had been woken twice in the night—once when a particularly large species of moth had somehow invaded the children's room, and secondly when David awoke, terrified at the strangeness of his surroundings.

But all that had happened several hours ago now, Caroline realised, as the heat of her room and the activity of her thoughts brought her fully awake. As yet, no one seemed to be stirring in the apartment, but the brilliance of the sunlight which was penetrating even the shutters of her windows was sufficient to arouse her to a full awareness of exactly where she was. And besides, there was a distinctly alien lack of inhibition about the noises coming from outside the hotel.

She thrust back the cotton sheet which had suddenly become too heavy on her slender limbs and slid out of bed. Her feet appreciated the coolness of the floor tiles as she went to the window, but when she thrust the shutters wide the heat caused her to draw back into the shadows as her eyes adjusted themselves.

Her windows overlooked the side of the hotel and immediately below she could identify the noises she had heard. Three stories below were the hotel kitchens and from there came the clatter of dishes and the shouted commands of someone in charge. Dustbin lids clattered as black-skinned houseboys in white shirts and shorts covered by long aprons came to empty rubbish, and an assortment of mangy dogs hung about the outer precincts obviously hoping for scraps.

Beyond the less salubrious environs of the kitchen yard

a stretch of browned grass gave on to the road down which they had travelled the night before. Although there was quite a lot of traffic using it now it was a much more motley collection than Caroline was used to seeing from the windows of her London flat. There were carts and bicycles, fruit and vegetable drays drawn by oxen, and lorries and cars thickly smeared with dust. Although the road itself was smoothly surfaced, there were no pavements to speak of, just mud-baked paths at the side along which moved a steady stream of women and children. The women carried baskets of clothes or produce on their heads, and Caroline could only assume they were going to the market. This unsophisticated view of humanity went oddly with the skyscraper blocks of hotels and offices and other commercial buildings which formed the nucleus of this apparently thriving African capital.

Turning back into her bedroom, Caroline tried to dispel a sense of disappointment. After all, she had chosen to come to Tsaba, no one had forced her to do it, and just because it was far removed from the picturesque jungle clearing of her imagination it did not mean that she regretted coming. On the contrary, her surroundings were immaterial. She was here to do a job of work, and if by chance she should get to meet Gareth, well ...

There was only one bathroom to serve the whole suite, so as everyone else seemed to be sleeping on Caroline made the most of it. She took a shower, smoothed a perfumed anti-sunburn cream into her arms and legs, and brushed her hair until it shone. Her hair was her best feature, she thought. Thick and lustrous, it swung in a dark chestnut curtain to her shoulders where it tilted under, curving confidingly under her chin in front. She was not unaware that amber eyes edged by long thick lashes and a wide, attractive mouth gave one a distinctly appealing appearance, but

7

she had never considered herself beautiful. She was too tall, she thought. Girls who were five feet seven inches in their stockinged feet could never appear weak and clinging, and while she could get away with strongly coloured dramatic clothes, the envy of some of her friends, frilly, feminine garments did not suit her.

After her shower, she dressed in slim-fitting cotton pants in a rather unusual shade of lilac, and a sleeveless yellow tank top. By the time she returned to her room she could hear David and Miranda arguing and when she reached the door of their room Miranda burst into tears. As soon as she saw Caroline, she rushed across to her, wrapping her arms around Caroline's thighs and clinging to her.

Caroline released the little girl's arms and went down on her haunches beside her. 'Now what's going on?' she asked gently.

'She's just a baby,' remarked David, with all the disgust of a seven-year-old describing a five-year-old. 'I only said there'd be spiders at La Vache!'

'Oh, David!' Caroline gave him an impatient look.

'He—he didn't just s-say that!' stammered Miranda, drawing back to look with tear-wet eyes into Caroline's face. 'He—he said they'd—they'd be 'normous ones and they'd— they'd come into my bed at night!'

Caroline rose to her feet and faced her eldest charge. 'Oh, he did, did he? Well, that was clever of you, wasn't it, David? Frightening a little girl. And not just any little girl. Your sister!'

David had the grace to look a little shamefaced. 'It was only a joke,' he muttered into the neck of his pyjamas.

'And I suppose it was a joke last night when you woke up, terrified and shouting for Mummy?'

David hunched his shoulders. 'That was different,' he exclaimed, colouring, as Miranda's eyes turned in his direction. 'I—I had a nightmare.'

'And don't you think what you've been telling Miranda is enough to give her nightmares?'

'I s'pose so.'

'Right. Then let's have no more of it.' Caroline looked back down at Miranda. 'All right now?'

Miranda shook her head. 'But are there spiders at La Vache?' she persisted.

Caroline sighed. 'Miranda, there are spiders everywhere. There needs to be. They're very useful creatures.'

'How? How are they useful?' David scrambled off his bed to come across and join them.

Caroline seated herself patiently on Miranda's bed and was explaining the role of the spider to her intrigued listeners when a slim, negligée-clad figure drifted through the open doorway.

Elizabeth Lacey, Caroline's employer, was almost thirty but looked younger. Small and vulnerable in appearance, she belonged to that breed of women who seem incapable of managing even the most uncomplicated of tasks, and Elizabeth traded on it. Caroline, who had known Elizabeth for several years before becoming her employee, knew perfectly well that should it suit her, Elizabeth could tackle anything; but as she had a husband who was susceptible to reproachful looks from wide blue eyes and who continually felt guilty that his work should constantly take him away from his family, she managed to avoid anything closely approaching exerting herself. In England, her mother was her standby, or unpaid housekeeper, thought Caroline with reluctant candour, but when it had come to leaving England, to spending several weeks in Africa, even her mother had drawn the line.

And that was where Caroline had come in. The spring term was at an end, she could afford to take a decrease in salary, it suited her to be out of touch for a while, and besides, Elizabeth's husband worked in Tsaba.

Now Elizabeth flexed her neck muscles tiredly, and said: 'What time is it? My watch hasn't been adjusted yet.'

Caroline glanced at the broad masculine watch on her wrist.

'A little after nine,' she replied. 'Are you hungry?'

'Hungry?' exclaimed Elizabeth, aghast. 'No——'

'I am!'

'I am!'

Two eager voices drowned what their mother had been about to say, and Elizabeth looked at them reprovingly.

'Do you mind?' she said, putting a languid hand to her head. 'I have a headache. Do try and behave like polite children and not hooligans!'

Any two children less like hooligans Caroline could not have imagined, but she put Miranda firmly off her knee and rose to her feet. 'Aren't you feeling any better, Elizabeth?'

Elizabeth sighed. 'It's so hot, isn't it?' Then she seemed to gather herself. 'Has Charles called yet?'

Caroline shook her head. 'I expect he's giving you time to rest before disturbing you,' she comforted.

Elizabeth's blue eyes hardened. 'I should have thought he could have made the effort to be at the airport last night instead of leaving us in the hands of—of—foreigners!'

Caroline glanced at the children, realising they were listening to every word of this exchange. 'You know perfectly well that it was impossible for him to leave La Vache yesterday, Elizabeth,' she said, guiding the other woman out of the children's bedroom. 'Go get washed, you two,' she added over her shoulder. 'Then we'll have something to eat.'

In her own bedroom, Elizabeth was quite happy to be

helped back into bed. 'You're so capable, Caroline,' she sighed, resting back against her pillows. 'I'm so glad you agreed to come with us. I don't know how I should have managed in this dreadful place without someone to help with the children.'

'You relax,' advised Caroline, straightening the bedclothes. 'The children and I will go down to the restaurant for breakfast. Shall I have you something sent up?'

Elizabeth blinked. 'Well—perhaps some coffee,' she conceded. 'And do you suppose one can get toast here?'

'I'll see.' Caroline's lips twitched. 'You just rest and leave everything to me.'

'But what about Charles? Do you think perhaps you should telephone him——'

'Charles will get in touch with you when he's able,' replied Caroline firmly. She walked towards the door. 'You'll be all right?'

Elizabeth plucked at the sheet. 'I suppose so. Caroline, you do think I was right to come out here, don't you? I mean—well, what do you think La Vache will be like?'

Caroline hesitated. 'Your place is with your husband, Elizabeth. And if his work is in some Central African state then that's where you should be.'

'Oh, I couldn't live here!' Elizabeth was horrified.

'No one's asking you to live here,' retorted Caroline calmly. 'Just to spend a few weeks with your husband because he's unable to come to England and spend them with you.'

Elizabeth nodded. 'I suppose you're right.' But she didn't sound convinced.

'Now look,' said Caroline, 'if my husband spent the better part of nine months of the year away from me, I'd have to do something about it.'

'Would you?' Elizabeth's eyes narrowed. 'Like not getting married, for example?'

Caroline flushed now. 'I don't know what you mean.'

'Oh, yes, you do, Caroline.' Elizabeth didn't look half so defenceless when she was on the attack. 'As soon as you discovered that Gareth Morgan had no intention of giving up his overseas appointment and settling to an office job in London, you turned him down—*flat*!'

'Elizabeth, I was only seventeen——'

'That doesn't matter. You had more sense than to tie yourself to an engineer with wanderlust in his veins instead of blood——'

'It wasn't like that——'

'Wasn't it?' Elizabeth sounded sceptical. 'I wonder what he's doing now? Gareth, I mean. Where he is? The last time I heard he was in charge of a hydro-electric project in Zambia——'

'I'll see about your toast and coffee.' Caroline refused to discuss the matter further.

Elizabeth was instantly contrite. 'Oh, Caroline, I haven't offended you, have I, darling?' she began, resuming an appealing tone.

'No, of course you haven't offended me,' exclaimed Caroline rather shortly, and went quickly, closing the door behind her.

But it was not so easy closing the door on her own thoughts. After all, there had been some truth in Elizabeth's allegations, even though the passage of time had served to nullify the less pleasant aspects of that situation seven years ago. She even felt a sense of guilt at not having told Elizabeth that she knew that Gareth Morgan was working in Tsaba now, building a dam on the River Kinzori not too many miles distant from La Vache. But how could she tell her that when she had no idea how Gareth would take her

12

presence in Tsaba, when he himself had no idea that she was coming?

Thrusting the difficulties she might have to face at some future date away from her, Caroline went in search of the children. Miranda was obediently putting on the cotton dress she had worn to travel in and Caroline made a mental note to find a sunsuit for her to wear after breakfast, but David, it appeared, had not yet come out of the bathroom and when Caroline went to see what he was doing she found him naked under the shower, and the floor swimming with water.

'Oh, David!' she gasped in exasperation, quickly kicking off her sandals to walk barefooted through the pools of water to turn off the shower. 'Go and get dressed at once before I find a more painful method to put a tan on your small bottom!'

David giggled and grabbing a towel edged his way out of the bathroom, leaving Caroline to mop the floor. Fortunately the tiles soon dried, and she emerged in time to prevent the children going into their mother's room.

'Mummy's resting,' she explained quietly. 'We're going down to the restaurant to have our breakfast, and then later on I expect Daddy will telephone and let us know how and when we can go to La Vache.'

Miranda tugged at her short fair curls which were so much like her mother's. 'Will it be today?' she asked excitedly. 'Will we see Daddy today?'

'Possibly.' Caroline didn't want to raise their hopes too high. 'La Vache is all of seventy miles from here, and the roads aren't like our roads in England. They're just tracks after you leave the city behind.'

'How do you know?' asked David, practical as ever. His hair was plastered to his head now, but Caroline thought that in this heat it wouldn't take long to dry. She herself was already sweating from the mild exertion of mopping up the bathroom floor and she dreaded to think how Elizabeth would cope if she was expected to do anything physical.

But now she said: 'I've read books. And I know what your daddy has told us when he's been home on leave. Besides, if you knew a little more about the climate you'd realise that things don't stay the same here as they do back home.'

She saw that Miranda was frowning at this and as they traversed the wide corridor to the lifts she tried to explain how lush and luxuriant was the vegetation that could overnight undo the work of the day. In truth, she found it hard to accept herself. She had never witnessed the destructive power of liana creepers, strangling the life out of struggling undergrowth, entwining trees together into an impassable living mesh that had to be hacked away with machetes. And yet it did happen, and the children were morbidly fascinated by her revelations.

Downstairs, a wide hall with an enormous revolving fan opened into the various public rooms of the hotel. Flowering, climbing plants rioted over low ornamental trellises, while huge stone urns spilled exotically coloured lilies and flame flowers over the cool, marble-tiled floor. It was obvious that no expense had been spared in making the Hotel Ashenghi as attractive to its guests as was humanly possible in a climate verging constantly on the unbearable.

As Caroline paused to get her bearings she encountered the eye of a man who appeared to be the head waiter standing in the arched entrance to the restaurant, keeping his waiters under surveillance. He bowed courteously as she approached him, and asked if she required a table. His English was quite good, so Caroline thanked him, and after he had shown them to a table set in a window embrasure, she said:

'Mrs. Lacey—the children's mother—is not feeling well. She'd like some coffee in her suite, and would it be possible for her to have some toast?'

The head waiter smiled, his teeth startlingly white in his black face. 'Of course, madam. I will see to it myself. Now, what would you and these children like to eat?'

Caroline had coffee, but David and Miranda chose fruit juice, and they all tried the warm rolls spread with conserve. The butter that was provided in a dish of ice cubes wasn't to their taste and David, with his usual lack of discretion, said in a clear, distinct voice that it was rancid. Of course, it wasn't, but even Caroline preferred to avoid it. There was a dish of fruit on the table, too—mangoes and bananas, pawpaws and oranges, but Caroline advised the children to wait before trying anything too unfamiliar to their stomachs. All in all, it was an enjoyable meal, the fans set at intervals about the room creating a cooling draught which was most acceptable. Clearly, the air-conditioning kept the temperature down, but the fans helped to disperse the flies.

Judging by the number of used tables it appeared that by this hour of the morning most of the hotel's guests had already partaken of breakfast, and Caroline and the children were the last to leave. They were walking towards the lifts when a man who had been talking to the receptionist turned away from the desk and saw them. He was a tall man, lean and muscular, dressed in narrow fitting mud-coloured pants and a cream bush shirt, but what attracted Caroline's attention was the man's hair. It was corn-fair, streaked with a lighter shade, as though the sun had bleached it, and it was startling against the dark tan of his skin. She had only known one man with hair like that, one man whose ice-blue eyes could turn to green when he

15

was emotionally aroused, one man who had once asked her to marry him, and she had turned him down because she had youthfully asserted that she didn't intend to marry a penniless engineer and go and live in some awful, God-forsaken, undeveloped country. How stupid she had been, how careless with the one thing in her life she had ever really wanted . . .

The man was standing quite still now staring at her, and she moved uncomfortably under that intent scrutiny. But for a moment she had felt as shocked as he must be at seeing her here. What could he be thinking? What kind of a coincidence did he think this was?

Realising that it was up to her to make the first overture, she took a few steps towards him and said: 'Hello, Gareth. This is a surprise, isn't it?'

Gareth Morgan seemed to recover admirably quickly from his momentary pause. In fact, he didn't seem too shocked at all. It was Caroline who could feel the tremor of this encounter rushing through her veins, moistening her palms, sending a rivulet of sweat down her spine. She had not realised until then just how much she had wanted to see him again, and she had the most ridiculous impulse to run to him, to press herself against him, and beg his forgiveness for what happened seven years ago.

But of course the very fact that it was seven years ago precluded any show of emotion. Seven years was a long time, and a lot had happened—to both of them. Why else had she waited so long before making any attempt to contact him? Even now, facing him, the width of the years stretched between them, made even wider by the cold detachment on his face.

'So you really came, Caroline,' he remarked at last. 'I never believed you would.'

He made no attempt to take the hand that she had tentatively offered, and awkwardly she allowed her arm to drop to her side. She was aware of Miranda's speculative interest, of David's curiosity, and gathering all her composure, she said: 'I don't know what you mean.'

Gareth looked sceptical. 'No? Oh, well, never mind.'

Caroline frowned. 'Did you know I was coming, then?'

'Know? Of course I knew. I thought that was the general idea. I just can't imagine why you bothered.'

Caroline coloured. 'I'm afraid you're mistaken if you think I supplied advance notice of my arrival——' she began hotly.

'Am I?' Gareth's tone was mocking. 'Didn't you expect us to meet?'

Caroline bent her head to the children. 'Look!' she said. 'There's a monkey hiding in that tree just outside the window. Why don't you go and see what it does?'

David looked at Caroline and then at the tall man standing nearby. 'You're just wanting to get rid of us,' he declared, with his usual candour. 'Why? Who is this man? Does he work for Daddy?'

Caroline straightened, her cheeks burning now. This was hardly the way she had envisaged her first meeting with Gareth Morgan. She had thought to surprise him, and if she had hoped for any reaction from him it had not been this mocking derision and scarcely concealed contempt.

'Are these Lacey's children?' he asked now, and David said:

'I'm David Lacey, and this is my sister Miranda. Who are you?'

'My name is Gareth Morgan,' replied Gareth, his expression changing somewhat as he went down on his haunches beside them. 'I suppose you could call me a friend of your daddy's.'

'Do you live at La Vache, too?' asked Miranda.

17

Gareth shook his head. 'No. I live at a place called Nyshasa, but it's not far from La Vache. I live near the river.'

David's eyes were round. 'Are there crocodiles in the river? My teacher at school said there were crocodiles in Africa.'

'Oh, there are. But they prefer calmer waters than where I live. We do have hippos, though, and they're quite interesting.'

'How super!' David was enthralled. 'Do you think my daddy would take me to see them——'

'And me,' piped up Miranda, when Caroline interrupted them.

'Not now, children,' she exclaimed, realising the sharpness of her tone had less to do with them than with the man talking so casually to them. 'Er—I'm sure Mr. Morgan has more important things to do than waste his valuable time talking to us.'

Garth straightened, flexing his back muscles, unwillingly drawing Caroline's eyes to the broadness of his chest. He was leaner than she remembered, but no less attractive because of it. 'On the contrary,' he was saying mildly, 'I came here to meet you and take you back to La Vache.'

'What?' Caroline gasped, and then quickly tried to hide her astonishment. 'But—but I don't understand——'

'Nicolas Freeleng and I are old friends. Lacey told him that an old—acquaintance—of mine was coming out here with his wife to help her with the children. Then, when they ran into some trouble at the mine, and it was going to be difficult for Lacey to get away, Nick asked me whether I'd do it—seeing that we were old acquaintances.'

'I—I see.' Caroline digested this with reluctance. 'Well, I'm sorry if we're being an inconvenience to you.'

'Did I say you were?'

'No. No, but——'

'But what?' Gareth's eyes narrowed to thin slivers of blue ice. 'Wasn't this the way you intended us to meet? What did you hope to do, Caroline? Disarm me with surprise—and seduce me with what might have been?'

Caroline was shocked at the bitterness in his tone. 'Of course not,' she denied defensively. 'Surely after all these years we can meet as—as friends.'

'*Friends*?' There was pure contempt in his voice now. 'Caroline, you and I can never be friends, and you know it. Now, I don't know what you hoped to achieve by coming here—I imagined you'd be happily married to some comfortably-off business man by now. That was your intention, wasn't it?' His lip curled. 'I might even be doing you a disservice by suspecting that I figure in any way in your plans. But I'm giving you fair warning, if you have any foolish notion of entertaining yourself while you're here by trying to rekindle old fires, you'll be wasting your time!'

CHAPTER TWO

THE heat in the station wagon was intense, but to wind down the windows was to invite clouds of choking dust into the car, and therefore the heat was the lesser of the two evils. All the same, Caroline felt as though every inch of her body was soaked with sweat, and she wished David would stop bouncing about from side to side in his determination not to miss anything. Even Elizabeth, more comfortably ensconced in the front of the vehicle beside Gareth, fanned herself constantly with her handkerchief, and could no longer keep up the inconsequent chatter she had bubbled with when first they started off. Elizabeth was invariably at her best when in the company of an attractive man, and the fact that Gareth made only monosyllabic replies to her inane questions seemed to bother her not at all.

But the afternoon was wearing into early evening now, and the shadows were lengthening beside the mud-baked track. There was a dank smell of rotting vegetation from the jungle-like mass that encroached on the narrow road, and from time to time the shrill cry of some wild animal rent the dying afternoon air. Miranda had long since passed the excitable stage and now curled into her corner, persistently sucking her thumb in spite of Caroline's reprovals and David's jeering.

Caroline herself felt that her awareness of everything around her had been sharpened by the tension between herself and Gareth. Not that anyone else appeared to be aware of it. On the contrary, from the moment Elizabeth was introduced her only interest had been to draw his attention to herself.

Gareth had accompanied Caroline and the children up in the lift to Elizabeth's suite. After making his shattering statement in the hall of the hotel, he had diverted his attention to David and Miranda, and while Caroline had burned with resentment and a painful kind of humiliation, he had talked casually to the children about safaris he had made into nearby Tanzania, and the dramatic nature reserve of the Ngorongoro Crater. By the time they reached the suite David was completely won over, and Caroline did not have to introduce her employer to the tall, lean stranger: David did it for her.

Elizabeth's headache seemed to miraculously disappear. She immediately left her bed to seek the bathroom and when she emerged at last she had looked cool and feminine in a pale pink dress that clung to her shapely figure.

Caroline had spent the time that Elizabeth had taken to get ready standing nervously by the window, staring down desperately on to the yard below, willing the whole scene that had just taken place to have been some awful nightmare. But of course it was not. Gareth was there in the room with her, apparently indifferent to her presence, showing a boyish interest in the toys that both David and Miranda had produced for his inspection.

When Elizabeth finally had joined them, it had been worse. Caroline had had to listen to the other woman laughing about the fact that only that morning she and Caroline had been talking about him, and what a lovely surprise it was to find he was working in Tsaba now.

Gareth had responded courteously enough, but Caroline had sensed his desire to get away. He had advised them to have an early lunch, then rest on their beds, and he would come back for them at about four o'clock when the heat was beginning to wane. He cleverly evaded Elizabeth's

21

suggestion that he should have lunch with them, saying that he had business to attend to in Ashenghi, and then he left them with a polite smile, and a casual salute that was meant for David.

After he had gone, Caroline had had to face Elizabeth's questions. Had she known he was working in Tsaba? How had he reacted when he had found her in charge of the children? And what exactly did he do?

Caroline had parried them as best she could. Fortunately for her David was not paying a great deal of attention to their conversation. It was boring stuff after what Mr. Morgan had just been telling him, and so Caroline did not have to suffer his recollections of her confrontation with Gareth. Instead, she had allowed Elizabeth to assume that it had been as much a surprise to her as to anyone else meeting him like that, and therefore she was no wiser as to his present activities than she had been before. It had been a cowardly little subterfuge, she thought now, disgusted at her own duplicity, but the last thing she wanted was to give Elizabeth any reason to suspect that she had come here for any other reason than to help out a friend in need. What small portion of pride that was left to her must remain intact or she might be tempted to funk the whole thing and take the next flight back to England.

It was dark by the time they reached La Vache and thousands of insects were visible in the headlights' glare, dying in their hundreds against the windscreen. An enormous moth hit the car with a sickening thud, leaving a trail of fluid to run unheeded down the glass, and Caroline felt slightly nauseated. Last night, driving to the hotel, she had been tired but excited, eager to experience the thinly-veneered primitiveness that was Africa. But tonight she felt bruised and uncertain, more convinced as every moment passed that she was going to regret coming here.

La Vache was a collection of houses, built for the white population, and adjoining a sort of village compound. In the half light thrown from lighted windows, Caroline glimpsed an open fire and a collection of curious black faces turned in their direction before Gareth swung between some trees and brought the station wagon to a halt before a corrugated-roofed bungalow. Almost before the vehicle's engine ground to a halt a door was thrown open and a man dressed in white shirt and shorts came hurrying down the shallow steps towards them. Gareth had got out of the car before the other man reached them, but it was obvious that the newcomer had eyes for no one but Elizabeth.

Caroline levered herself stiffly out of the back of the station wagon, trying to avoid watching the languid way Elizabeth responded to Charles's enthusiastic welcome, and was glad when the children scrambled out and broke it up, shouting: 'Daddy! Daddy! We're here!'

Ignoring the hand that Gareth had offered to help her out of the vehicle, Caroline stood on the hard track, flexing her aching muscles, and looking about her with reluctant interest. Her first impressions were of the closeness of the community, and a certain sense of claustrophobic unease at the encroaching forest. Was this her jungle clearing? Was this to be the romantic communion with nature which had sounded so delightful when viewed from a distance? It all seemed so different, so primitive and yet perversely prosaic somehow. And that smell of rotting vegetation—one didn't learn about things like that from books.

Gareth was unloading their suitcases from the back of the station wagon. Caroline supposed she should be helping him. After all, that was why she was here, wasn't it? To help! But right now, she felt as though she was the one who needed to be helped, and there was no one to do it. For the first time since leaving England she thought rather

23

nostalgically about the comfortable relationship she had shared with Jeremy Brent, and wondered whether he would accept the severance of their engagement as she had insisted he should.

Then Charles turned from his family and gave her a warm, comforting smile. 'Good to see you again, Caroline,' he said. 'Glad you made it.' Then he turned to Gareth: 'I'm in your debt, Morgan. Come along inside and we'll all have a drink to celebrate.'

Gareth made a deprecating gesture. 'Thanks, but I can't stop,' he demurred. 'I've got to get back to Nyshasa.'

'Oh, must you?' That was Elizabeth, and even the children echoed her disappointment. Only Caroline said nothing, made no effort to detain him.

Gareth shook his head. 'I'm sorry. But I have been away since early this morning. Some other time, perhaps.'

'Oh, yes, you must come and have dinner with us one evening while we're here, mustn't he, Charles?' exclaimed Elizabeth.

'Of course, of course,' Charles smiled. 'I'll be in touch, Morgan.'

'You do that.'

Gareth nodded pleasantly and walked round the station wagon to get into the driving seat again. He had to pass Caroline to do so and for a brief moment hard blue eyes bored into hers. Deliberately she assumed a defiant stance, returning his gaze challengingly, refusing to let him see that he could in any way disconcert her, and then he was past and climbing into the vehicle, raising his hand in farewell to the others. The engine fired, he let in his clutch, put the car into gear and it moved smoothly away. Only then did Caroline realise that she had been holding her breath for fully one minute.

'Come along, Caroline.' Charles ushered his family

24

across the stretch of dried grass that formed a sort of garden at the front of the bungalow. 'Thomas has a meal all ready for you.'

Thomas turned out to be Charles's houseboy. He had a permanently smiling face, and the children took to him at once. Also, Charles explained, it made it very difficult for one to chastise him. It was impossible to remain angry for long with someone who looked so cheerfully innocent.

Before sitting down to their meal, Charles suggested that they might like to familiarise themselves with the layout of the bungalow, and as the children were keen, Elizabeth agreed. The building was divided into two halves by a long, narrow hall that ran from front to back. On one side was the large lounge-cum-dining area, with a small bedroom at the back where Caroline was to sleep; and on the other were the two larger bedrooms where Charles and Elizabeth, and the children were to sleep. The bathroom, like the kitchen, was annexed to the back of the bungalow, and comprised of a chipped wash basin and rather primitive toilet, with a shower that could only be used if an overhead tank had first been manually filled.

The children found this tour of inspection fascinating, and Miranda had cast away the slightly dejected air she had worn during the latter stages of their journey. The sight of the mosquito nets draped above their beds made the prospect of sleeping so much more exciting, and David asserted that he was going to take a shower the very next day.

But Caroline could see Elizabeth's face changing as she began to appreciate the lack of facilities. The bungalow bore no resemblance to the comfort of the hotel in Ashenghi, and perhaps it was a pity that they had had to spend a night there. The contrast would not have been so much in evidence if they had driven on to La Vache last night. The furniture, for instance, was starkly practical, and because

25

there had been no feminine hand in the design there was not even a brightly patterned cushion to add colour to the dull browns and beiges that made up most of the curtains and upholstery.

However, the meal that Thomas had prepared was waiting for them and it fortunately precluded any immediate discussion of their surroundings. Introducing a new topic to divert Elizabeth's attention, Caroline asked what education was provided for the African children.

'It's quite good, actually,' replied Charles, obviously enjoying the somewhat stringy beef that Thomas had served together with beans and sweet potatoes. 'There's a mission only a mile away at Katwe Fork, and the padre's wife, Helen, teaches the younger children. The padre teaches the older children himself, and if by the time they reach eleven or twelve they show potential, he arranges for them to be transferred to the school at Luanga.'

Miranda choked then, and had to be thumped vigorously on the back by her brother before she could dislodge the piece of meat from her throat. Her eyes were streaming with tears by the time she coughed it up, as much with the hardness of David's pounding as with the shock of choking. But before Caroline could say anything to comfort her, Elizabeth turned on her husband:

'My God, Charles,' she exclaimed tremulously, 'I hope you're satisfied! Bringing us out to this dreadful place and expecting us to stay for weeks! Why, the food's not even edible, and you don't care that we might all die of dysentery or worse in these appalling conditions!' She flung her napkin down on the table and rose to her feet, ignoring Miranda's wail of: *'Mummy! Mummy!'* and marched to the door. 'I'm going to bed, and don't you dare to try and stop me!'

Apart from Miranda snuffling unhappily into her napkin

there was complete silence for several minutes after Elizabeth had left the room. Charles looked absolutely staggered, and Caroline felt terribly sorry for him. Obviously, in the excitement of their arrival he had not noticed Elizabeth's lack of enthusiasm, and her outburst had been completely unexpected so far as he was concerned.

At last it was David who broke the silence by saying: 'What's the matter with Mummy? What was she talking about? We're not going to die, are we, Daddy?'

Charles's mouth worked nervously. 'No—no, of course you're not going to die, son!' He put a slightly unsteady hand on David's head. 'I—er—I expect it's all the travelling. Mummy's tired, that's all, like she said. She'll feel better in the morning. Won't she, Caroline?'

As he looked across the table at her, Caroline realised that he was looking for reassurance, too, just as David had been. Poor Charles, he hadn't the faintest idea of how to deal with someone like Elizabeth. The trouble was he had always been too soft with her, too gentle and considerate. Living apart for most of the year as they did he was inclined to indulge her in everything when he came home, and Elizabeth had never known what it was to be thwarted. What she needed was a firmer hand, a less understanding nature; someone who would mete out to her the kind of treatment she usually allotted to other people. But whether Charles had it in him to adopt that kind of attitude towards his wife, Caroline had her doubts.

Now she said: 'I think we're all tired, Charles. And I shouldn't let what Elizabeth says bother you. It's all so different, you see. It takes time to get used to.'

Charles pushed his plate aside, his appetite obviously deserting him. 'I haven't noticed you making too much fuss,' he remarked, swallowing a mouthful of the lager which Thomas had provided to have with their meal.

Caroline smiled wryly. 'I don't have anyone to fuss at,' she replied cheerfully. 'Now, David, Miranda—who's going to try this blancmange that Thomas has made for us?'

Charles fidgeted his way through the sweet course which even Caroline had to admit was not very palatable. Made with dried milk, the blancmange was still powdery, and both David and Miranda refused to finish theirs. But when Thomas brought in the coffee, Charles rose to his feet.

'Look here, Caroline,' he exclaimed awkwardly, 'will you excuse me? I mean—well, I really think I ought to go and see if Elizabeth's all right ...'

Caroline nodded. 'That's all right, Charles. You go ahead. The children and I can manage perfectly well.'

Charles breathed a sigh of relief, bestowed a warm smile on his two youngsters, and then made a hasty exit.

'Why can't we go with Daddy?' asked Miranda, still rather tearful.

David nudged her in the ribs with his elbow. 'Don't be stupid, baby! They don't want us. They want to kiss and cuddle and that sort of thing, don't they, Caroline?'

Caroline hid a smile. 'If you say so, David,' she answered mildly, pouring herself another cup of coffee.

Later, Caroline got the children ready for bed while Thomas was clearing the table, and then, with his assistance, settled them beneath their mosquito nets. Fortunately Thomas spoke very good English although his manner of phrasing things wasn't always right, and she was glad of his help. She dreaded to think what would happen if either of the children wanted to go to the bathroom during the night. However would they manage to get back beneath their mosquito nets? She shook her head. Oh, well! That was a problem they would have to face if and when the occasion occurred.

Neither Charles nor Elizabeth had reappeared, and Caroline hoped that this was a good sign. At any rate, Elizabeth hadn't made another scene and turned him out of the bedroom.

After that, the bungalow was very quiet. Thomas had wished her goodnight and left for some private destination of his own, and Caroline sat in the lounge for a while wondering what one did in the evenings here. It was scarcely nine o'clock and yet bed seemed the only sensible conclusion.

Turning out the lights, she eventually went to her own cubbyhole of a room. Thomas had left her suitcase standing at the foot of the bed, and she lifted it on to a plain stinkwood chest that would apparently have to serve as a storage container for her underwear. The only other furniture in the room, apart from the iron-framed bed, was a tall hanging-closet, which, when she opened the door, smelt so strongly of disinfectant that she was deterred from hanging anything inside; and a kind of marble-topped washstand, on which stood a basin and a jug of rather brackenish-coloured water in which floated a motley assortment of flying insects. The floor was covered by a kind of cheap linoleum, and there was a rag rug beside the bed. All in all, it was not a very inspiring apartment, but at least the bed felt comfortable when she bounced on it.

Scooping away most of the insects, she managed to rinse her face and hands before taking off her clothes and putting on her nightdress. Quite honestly, she wished she had brought some pyjamas with her. There was something rather vulnerable about a nightdress when one couldn't be sure that one's bed might not be invaded by ants in the night.

Thrusting such disquieting thoughts aside, she turned out the light and climbed into bed. She supposed Elizabeth ought to be grateful that there was electric light here, run from a community generator. They could quite easily have found themselves with only oil lighting and no kind of refrigeration for food.

Lying there in the darkness, Caroline found her thoughts turning back to her meeting with Gareth Morgan. She had known this would happen, and that was why she had been loath to go to bed, but sooner or later she had to face the fact that whatever he had once felt for her, now he despised her and any crazy ideas she had had about effecting a reconciliation should be forgotten.

All the same, her reasons for coming here had not changed. The pity of it was that she had been unable to come any sooner. Anything she said now he would disbelieve even were he prepared to listen, which he so obviously was not. Why was it that one never recognised the value of something until it was out of reach?

She rolled on to her stomach, burying her face in the pillow. Could she ever be excused for her behaviour of seven years ago? She had only been seventeen years old, after all, whereas Gareth had been thirty even then. Perhaps that was why he had been so easily deterred. Perhaps he had considered himself too old for her. But it hadn't been that. It had been her own stupid belief that without a secure background—without money—no love could hope to survive. From an early age her mother had drilled it into her —the old adage: *when poverty comes in the door, love flies out of the window*. And she had believed it, believed it blindly. Hadn't her own father left her mother when she was small for those very reasons? Hadn't he taken off with some flighty young thing who had a job of her own and wouldn't saddle him with a home and family to support? Hadn't she seen the marriages of people around who were finding it hard to make ends meet and who indulged their frustrations in rows? And she had determined not necessarily to marry for money instead of for love, but rather only to love where money was.

Time had passed, changing things, changing Caroline's ideas, and bringing with it the realisation of exactly what she had lost. But by then it had been too late to regress. Gareth had placed himself out of her reach, and she had had to go on alone and make a life for herself.

And she had succeeded admirably. She had gone to college and become a qualified teacher, obtaining for herself a good post at a large comprehensive school. She was well liked among the staff and popular with the pupils, and after her mother died two years ago she had managed to get a small flat and become independent. From time to time she had had word of Gareth. His married sister lived in Hampstead, not far from where Caroline and her mother had lived, and whenever Caroline went back to visit old friends she had heard of Gareth through them.

Eventually, the thing that Caroline had once wanted to happen became reality. Through the headmaster at the school, she became friendly with Jeremy Brent, the headmaster of a well-established boys' preparatory school in Kensington. He was everything she had once looked for in a husband—rich and attractive, of a good family with excellent prospects, and what was more would inherit his father's baronetcy one day. He was instantly attracted to her and lost no time in asking her out and showing his interest was serious. Caroline should have been delighted, she should have been proud that a man like Jeremy wanted her for his wife, but something stopped her from falling in love with him. She knew that some part of her still hankered after a man who within a year of their separation had married and was still married to someone else. She used to tell herself that she was a fool, that if she wasn't careful she'd end up like her mother, a lonely and embittered woman, but

31

nevertheless, although she became engaged to Jeremy she delayed the inevitability of marriage.

Naturally, Jeremy became impatient. There was absolutely no reason why they should not get married right away. As well as his service flat in town, and his apartments at the school, he owned a small house in Sevenoaks which would suit them ideally until they started a family. He offered her a cruise to the West Indies for their honeymoon, and an unlimited account at Harrods to buy her trousseau. But still Caroline hesitated.

And then, early in the New Year, she had learned that Gareth's wife had left him, that they were getting a divorce, and suddenly she had known that this was why she had been delaying her marriage to Jeremy.

She had half expected that Gareth would come home, to England. She knew his parents were dead, but there was his married sister in Hampstead who hadn't seen him for years. But Gareth didn't come to England, and as the weeks passed Caroline had become impatient and restless. Then, when the opportunity arose to accompany Elizabeth Lacey and her children out to Tsaba, she had not hesitated. She had told Jeremy the truth—that she was very much afraid she loved someone else—and that before settling down with him she had to make sure.

Jeremy had not seemed too surprised. He had sensed for weeks that something was troubling her, but when it came to her giving him back his ring he became obstinate. He insisted that he was convinced this was just a phase she was going through, that when she got out to Africa and met this man again she would realise how foolish she had been, that no emotion she had felt when she was still a schoolgirl could possibly survive her maturity to womanhood.

However, Caroline could be obstinate too when she chose, and she had made him take back the ring.

'Who knows?' she had commented lightly, 'in the six weeks I'm away, you might meet someone far more worthy of your love than I am.'

'Don't be facetious!' Jeremy had snapped, snatching her in his arms and pressing his lips to hers. 'I won't let you go like this. I won't let you leave the country without the badge of my possession on your finger.'

'But you don't possess me,' Caroline had replied, rather quietly, and Jeremy had become angry.

'Perhaps I should have done,' he had exclaimed furiously. 'Perhaps if you were already mine, this fellow wouldn't want you anyway. Or were you his possession first?'

Caroline had slapped his face then. She had been unable to prevent herself and Jeremy had had the grace to look ashamed. 'I'm sorry, I'm sorry, Caroline,' he had cried frustratedly, 'but can't you see? I can't bear to let you go!'

But of course he had had to, although he had threatened that if she was not back within the six weeks she had promised, he would come out to Tsaba and fetch her back himself.

Caroline rolled on to her back and stared unseeingly up at the darkened roof above her. From time to time, she could hear rustlings outside the bungalow, and her flesh crept at the possibilities these noises conjured up. But mostly there were just the sounds of the night—the incessant scraping of the insects, the harsh croaking of bullfrogs, and occasionally the startled cry of some wild thing caught by a predator.

What was she doing here? she asked herself honestly. What was driving her to remain here and possibly risk further humiliation? What if Jeremy's turned out to be the love she craved and he grew tired of waiting for her? What would she do?

The answers were simple but stark. She was here because

33

in spite of everything she was still attracted to a man who had shown that his feelings for her had soon been replaced by those for another. And if Jeremy got tired of waiting, if he found someone else in her absence, then she hoped he would be happy. Because she very much doubted her ability to make herself happy, let alone anyone else . . .

CHAPTER THREE

CAROLINE slept badly. She tossed and turned in the narrow bed, occasionally stubbing her toes on the unaccustomed rails at its foot, and was awakened with a start at half past six by an uproar from the children's room. Only half awake, she sprang out of bed, searching for the quilted cotton robe she had draped over the chest the night before. The children's room was across the passage and as she emerged from her room she could hear Miranda screaming and David whooping exuberantly.

Wondering how on earth Charles and Elizabeth could sleep through such a din, she thrust open the children's door. Miranda was a quivering heap in one corner of the room, while her brother was bouncing excitedly up and down on his bed.

'What on earth is going on here?' Caroline demanded.

But even as she spoke she saw what it was that had reduced Miranda to a frightened jelly. Standing squarely on the floor between her and the comparative safety of her bed was a lizard, perhaps six inches in length, with grotesquely revolving eyes.

Miranda had stopped screaming at Caroline's entrance and pointed with trembling fingers towards the small reptile. 'It—it's a dragon!' she announced, her voice trembling. 'A baby dragon. And—and soon its mummy is going to come and take it away!'

Caroline gave David an impatient glance. 'Oh, really?' she commented. 'I suppose your brother told you that.'

Miranda started to nod, but David broke in, his expression indignant. 'No, I did not,' he denied. 'I only said that—

well, perhaps it might be a dragon . . .'

'But you knew it was not,' stated Caroline, turning to him. 'Didn't you?'

David hunched his shoulders. 'How should I know what it is?'

Caroline regarded the terrified creature with a certain amount of distaste. 'Well, Miranda, it's not a dragon. Nor is it a baby anything. It's a lizard, that's all. A harmless, frightened lizard, who can't understand what all this fuss is about. Can you see the way its little body is throbbing? That's because it's scared—more scared of you than you should be of it.'

Miranda scrambled slowly to her feet, her eyes glued to the creature as she did so. Then she looked across at Caroline. 'But—but what's it doing in here? How—how did it get in?'

David looked as though he was about to make some startling explanation, but then thought better of it when he met Caroline's cautioning stare. Caroline herself was trying desperately to think of some satisfactory explanation, but everything that occurred to her left the way open for Miranda to ask whether it might happen again. At last she decided to use the truth in a way that might relieve Miranda's mind.

'Well, ' she began carefully, 'I expect Mr. Lizard was taking his morning stroll when he found himself passing through this room. And then you started screaming and David started shouting, and poor old Mr. Lizard thought: My goodness me, there must be something terrible going on here. I'd better not go any farther in case I get involved.'

Miranda frowned. 'You mean—you mean he—usually comes through our bedroom?'

Caroline licked her lips which had suddenly gone dry. 'Well—er—yes—and no!' She paused, aware of David watching her closely. 'I expect sometimes he comes this way, and sometimes he goes some other way, but today just happened to be the day for the Laceys' bungalow.'

Miranda suddenly let out another little scream as the lizard, clearly tired of waiting any longer, darted swiftly towards the window, ran up the wall and disappeared through the shutters. Even Caroline could not completely hide the desire to gather her skirts more closely about her legs, but at least now it had gone and the atmosphere eased considerably.

'There you are,' she managed, with as much nonchalance as she could muster. 'He's gone, and after today's performance I doubt very much whether he'll want to come back.'

Miranda breathed a sigh of relief, and David sat cross-legged on his bed, watching her as she picked her way gingerly across the linoleum.

'I'm glad I'm not frightened of lizards,' he remarked disparagingly. 'I expect there are millions of them here——'

'David!' Caroline's tone was sharp. 'I will not have you deliberately frightening your sister like this! Now, I'm going to make some tea. If you two want to come along, you can. But put on your dressing gowns—and please be quiet! I don't want to wake your mother and father.'

'Oh, Daddy's gone,' remarked David airily. 'He left about half an hour ago.'

Caroline frowned. 'Left? For where?'

'For work,' he said. 'He came in to say goodbye to us. They start terribly early here because it's too hot to work later on.'

That made sense. Caroline nodded. 'Well, don't wake your mother, then,' she advised dryly.

'I expect Miranda's done that already,' replied David practically, and Caroline gave him another exasperated look before turning along the passage towards the kitchen.

She filled the kettle from the tap which Charles had explained the night before was attached to a large water tank outside. When the tank was empty, it had to be refilled from the nearby stream, and if it should rain, water was collected in barrels to be used as well. Plugging in the kettle, Caroline felt her spirits reasserting themselves. In spite of her broken night's sleep, things seemed infinitely brighter this morning. It was all an adventure, and in spite of his attitude towards her yesterday, the knowledge that Gareth Morgan was only a few miles away filled her with an unreasoning excitement.

While the kettle was boiling she took her first real look at La Vache. From the kitchen windows there was little to interest her in a patch of scrubby grass and a belt of jungle-like undergrowth, although the purple-shadowed mountains beyond had a remote beauty. But the living-room windows overlooked the lawn at the front of the house, and beyond it the hard-baked track which served as a road.

It was much bigger than Caroline remembered from the night before, with perhaps a dozen bungalows similar to the Laceys' set at intervals beside the track. It seemed strange to see smoke rising from open fires in the African village when already the sun was spreading a golden rose colour over everything and washing the white-painted buildings with it warmth. Across the track, in the garden of the house opposite, a tall flowering tree drooped orangey-red blossoms, strange and exotic, a reminder of the burning heat of the sun at noon. A movement near the tree distinguished itself as a white-throated monkey, and a smile lifted the corners of Caroline's mouth. The beauty she had sought to find in Ashenghi, and which had proved so elusive, was here in plenty if one chose to look for it, and only the whistling of the kettle dragged her away from her contemplation.

By the time David and Miranda appeared, Caroline had found cups and a teapot, set them on a tray, and was on her way back to Elizabeth's room. Making as little noise as possible, she opened Elizabeth's bedroom door, but then saw that her employer was awake.

Elizabeth lay on her back, the mosquito net thrust aside, staring broodingly up at the fly-marked ceiling above her head. When Caroline entered, her eyes turned in her direction and widened appreciatively when she saw the tray of tea. Struggling up on her pillows, she patted the bed beside her, and Caroline went forward and put down the tray, bending to pour tea for both of them.

David and Miranda hovered near the doorway. They knew better than to come bounding into their mother's bedroom without first ascertaining what kind of mood she was in, and although she was sipping her tea with evident enjoyment, Elizabeth did not look particularly happy.

'Charles has gone,' she remarked unnecessarily. 'He must have woken the children as well as me before he left, because there's been the most ghastly racket coming from their bedroom ever since.'

Caroline glanced at the children, still hesitating beside the door, and took pity on them. She felt like asking why, if Elizabeth had heard Miranda screaming, she hadn't gone to see what was the matter with her. Had she no maternal instincts whatsoever? But she decided against creating any more friction, and said instead:

'A lizard frightened Miranda, that was all. It ran away when I went in to them.'

'I see.' Elizabeth looked rather warily about the room as though expecting to find the unwelcome visitor in her room now, and then looked at her son and daughter. 'Well, come on in, if you're coming, can't you?' she cried irritably. 'You know I can't stand people who won't make up their minds what they're going to do!'

Miranda moved slowly over to her mother's bed. 'It was

the most 'normous lizard, Mummy,' she began, and then paused as David snorted derisively.

'It was not!' he declared. 'It was a harmless little thing, Caroline said so.'

'Yes, well, that's enough about the lizard,' said Caroline sharply. 'Miranda had a fright. But she's over it now.'

'I was very scared,' went on Miranda, clearly intent on deriving the maximum amount of sympathy from the incident, but Elizabeth wasn't listening to her.

'Charles said he'll be back as soon as he can,' she was explaining to Caroline. 'And in the meantime we're to have breakfast and look around.' She shuddered. 'Although what he expects us to look around at I can't imagine.'

'Oh, but there's lots to see,' replied Caroline, trying to arouse her enthusiasm. 'It's a wonderful morning, not too hot yet, and I've already seen the most beautiful tree in the garden opposite.'

'How exciting!' Elizabeth was sarcastic. 'Caroline, I'm beginning to wonder what kind of fool I've been in coming here! I mean—well, back home in England it all sounded quite easy—a holiday almost. But what kind of a holiday can anyone have when there's no hot water, hardly any bathing facilities, a houseboy who hasn't the first idea how to cook food, and no distinguishable sign of civilisation!'

'Try and look on it as an adventure,' said Caroline. 'After all, what's the point of coming to Africa and expecting it to be like an extension of England? It's not. There are no similarities, not in climate, or vegetation, or culture. You've got to take what there is and, for want of a better phrase, make the best of it.' She sighed. 'Oh, I know that sounds trite, but honestly, Elizabeth, there are more things in life than hot water and well-cooked food!'

Elizabeth's lips twisted. 'What a pity you're not Charles's wife, instead of me,' she remarked. 'The battle would have been won without a single shot being fired!'

Caroline bent her head. 'Why does there have to be a battle, Elizabeth? Heavens, Charles works here because he has to, because it's his way of providing for you and the children. The least you can do is try and see it his way. How would you have felt if Charles had come home on leave, turned his nose up at the meal you'd provided and then stormed off to bed like a child in a tantrum?'

'I think you've said enough, Caroline.' Elizabeth was beginning to look aloof, and Caroline realised she had gone too far. All the same, someone had to talk some sense into her, or she was going to make these six weeks purgatory for all of them.

'I'm only trying to make you see his side of things, Elizabeth,' she added quietly.

Elizabeth looked at her bent head, and then her expression softened. 'Oh, yes, I suppose you are,' she conceded at last. 'But I'm not like you, Caroline. I can't stand too much heat—or too much physical discomfort of any kind. I just go to pieces. My nerves simply won't support me.'

Caroline looked at her. 'We could all be a little like that,' she observed dryly. 'You don't suppose any of us are going to find it easy, do you? No. It's just that—well, at least keep an open mind. Don't prejudge everything. I think you might find there are compensations.' She hesitated. 'Surely it's good to be with Charles again?'

Elizabeth allowed a small smile to curve her lips. 'Oh, yes, I suppose that's true. All right, Caroline, I'll try and not show my feelings too blatantly, but don't expect miracles.'

Caroline smiled, 'I won't.'

By the time she had carried the tray back to the kitchen, washed in more of the tepid brown water in her bedroom, and dressed in a scarlet shirt and navy shorts, Thomas had

41

arrived to make breakfast. He greeted her with his usual good humour, obviously finding the sight of her long slender legs much to his liking.

Caroline left him to go and attend to the children. While they washed and cleaned their teeth she sorted through their clothes, putting most of their things away in a cedar-lined chest, similar to the one in her room. Then they dressed in tee-shirts and shorts, too, omitting their vests which had been a necessary item in April in London, but were superfluous here.

Breakfast comprised of rolls and fruit, very like what they had had the morning before in Ashenghi, and the coffee was every bit as good. Elizabeth had joined them, albeit in her dressing gown, and seemed to appreciate the simple meal. She drank several cups of strong black coffee with the cigarette she always enjoyed at this hour and looked more inclined to be affable afterwards. But when Caroline suggested that they might all take a walk later on, she shook her head vigorously.

'Not me, darling. I'm not dressed yet. But you three go, by all means. I'll be fine here. I'm going to ask Thomas whether I might take a shower, and then I'll accustom myself to my surroundings before Charles gets back. I might even supervise the cooking of our lunch.'

Caroline looked at the children's expectant faces and nodded. 'All right, we'll go. Perhaps it would be best anyway, just in case Charles returns while we're out.'

Some time later, walking along the sun-hard track that meandered its way between the bungalows of the European population towards the African village, Caroline was glad she had agreed to the outing. Although it was hot, the sun had not yet assumed the fiery sharpness that burned at midday. There was a haze of heat ahead of them that shimmered like a living thing, blurring the edges of their vision, and casting a sympathetic cloak over the harsher aspects of the settlement. It endeavoured to conceal the pitiful poverty of the mud dwellings that spread beyond the orderly rows of bungalows, the skeletal thinness of the few cattle which turned to regard them with mournful eyes, and the unpleasant lack of sanitation.

And yet, in spite of everything, the people themselves looked healthy, and happy, enough. The babies, who ran naked to their mothers at the appearance of this strange white woman and her children, had plump, rounded little bodies and bright, inquisitive eyes. There was a distinct absence of men to be seen, except for a few ancients seated cross-legged beside an open fire, smoking pipes and talking incessantly. Caroline assumed that all the able-bodied males were working, either at the mine or perhaps at some form of agriculture, although there seemed little scope for cultivation of crops about here. The women looked at them without interest, but Caroline was not disposed to linger. She felt that they were intruding somehow, and in spite of the children's disappointed protests, turned back the way they had come.

They were perhaps half way back to the bungalow, when a low-slung American limousine came cruising alongside and stopped just ahead of them. A man leaned out, a dark-haired, thick-set, handsome man, who smiled a greeting. Caroline stiffened. Surely they were not about to be accosted in this remote outpost?

However, to her surprise, the man knew their names. 'Hello,' he called. 'You look too young to be the children's mother, so you must be Miss Ashford, is that right? And that's David and Miranda.'

Caroline took a few tentative steps forward, holding both the children's hands firmly. 'Yes, I'm Caroline Ashford. But I'm afraid——'

43

'I know.' The man thrust open his door and climbed out, revealing that he was only a little taller than Caroline herself. 'You're naturally wondering who I am. Well, allow me to introduce myself. I'm Nicolas Freeleng. Gareth may have mentioned my name to you.'

At the mention of Gareth Morgan's name, a wave of hot colour swept into Caroline's cheeks. But of course the name was familiar. Wasn't it for Freeleng Copper Incorporated that Charles worked?

Allowing her fingers to be engulfed in the man's broad palm, Caroline managed to nod and say: 'Yes, I do recall your name, Mr. Freeleng. How do you do?'

'I'm very well, thank you.' He let her withdraw her hand from his rather reluctantly. 'I don't feel I have to ask you that question. You look quite—delightful, if I may say so.'

Caroline's colour did not subside as she introduced the children. Inevitably, David had a question and for once she was glad. While Nicolas Freeleng explained the dials on the car's dashboard to his enthralled listener, she had an opportunity to study the man.

He was quite young, much younger than she would have expected him to be, perhaps thirty-nine or forty, with square shoulders and a rather heavily-built body. He was dressed in khaki shirt and trousers, and there were already signs of perspiration on the shirt's crisp surface.

When he could extricate himself from David's curiosity, he turned back to Caroline, and said: 'Perhaps I can give you a lift back to Lacey's bungalow, Miss Ashford. Actually, I was on my way there to see Mrs. Lacey when I saw you. I was about to suggest that you all dine with me at my house this evening.'

Caroline glanced down at the children. 'I'm sure Mrs. Lacey will love that, Mr. Freeleng,' she replied. 'However, I hope you will understand that I couldn't accept your invitation myself.'

'Why not?' Nicolas's brows ascended.

'Well—because I'm here to look after the children——'

'If necessary the children can come, too,' declared Nicolas, with a certain amount of arrogance. 'I insist that you join us. You can't remain aloof in a community like ours, Miss Ashford. We all depend upon one another too much for that.'

Caroline sighed. 'It's not a question of remaining aloof, Mr. Freeleng——'

'Is it not? Then you will come.' He smiled suddenly. 'But we are wasting time. Come, get in the car. We'll go and see Mrs. Lacey. I'm sure she'll see it my way.'

Elizabeth was not about when they entered the bungalow, and excusing herself, Caroline left Nicolas with the children and went in search of her employer. She could hear Thomas singing in the kitchen as she went along the passage and a frown drew her dark brows together. Where was Elizabeth? Why hadn't she appeared when she heard them come in?

She knocked at her employer's bedroom door almost perfunctorily, and then her frown deepened as she heard Elizabeth call: 'Go away! I don't want anything!' in a harsh, grating voice.

Caroline hesitated, and then knocked again, and this time Elizabeth demanded who it was.

'It's me, Elizabeth. Caroline. Can I come in?'

'Oh, Caroline! Yes, yes, come on in. I thought it was that idiot Thomas.'

Caroline opened the door and entered the room and then stared at Elizabeth in surprise. She was still wrapped in her dressing robe, and she had not even bothered to comb her unruly curls.

'Why, Elizabeth!' she exclaimed. 'Why aren't you

45

dressed? I thought you were going to take a shower.'

That was obviously the wrong thing to say. Elizabeth flung herself off the bed where she had been lounging and glared at her. 'So I was,' she stated dramatically, 'so I was! And you may well ask why I haven't. I'll tell you! That idiot Thomas spent half an hour filling the water tank so that I could take a shower and then omitted to explain how the damn thing worked. Of course, I pulled this sort of release valve and the whole tank emptied itself, and there I was—wet, but unwashed. I asked him to fill it again, but he said he had other jobs he would have to do before Massa Lacey came home, and therefore, *I* would have to wait.'

This whole statement was issued with an immense amount of emphasis, and when Elizabeth had finished she flopped down on to the bed again as though she had spent herself.

'So?' she added. 'And how did you enjoy your walk?'

Caroline gathered herself. 'That's why I'm here, actually. You've got a visitor.'

'A visitor!' Elizabeth sprang up again. 'Why didn't you say so? Who is it?'

'You didn't give me much chance to say anything,' pointed out Caroline patiently. 'Actually it's Nicolas Freeleng.'

'*Nicolas Freeleng*!' The change in Elizabeth's demeanour was startling. 'Charles's boss?'

'Well, if he works for Nicolas Freeleng, yes, I suppose that's who it is.'

'Heavens!' Elizabeth tugged at her hair in an agony of despair. 'Oh, Caroline darling! Help me! Help me, please. You can't—you simply can't go out and tell him I'm not even dressed yet!'

'All right.' Caroline looked round. 'What do you want me

46

to do?'

Elizabeth began pouring water into the basin on a washstand exactly like the one in Caroline's bedroom. She waved a careless hand in the direction of her suitcases which had been opened the night before but the contents of which were simply strewn half in and half out.

'Find me something to wear, darling. Anything will do. That green linen—yes, that's the one. Undo the buttons for me, there's a love. I must just put on a little make-up.'

'I didn't bother,' remarked Caroline, automatically taking things out of the suitcases and placing them neatly in the drawers of a small chest. 'You'll find the heat will cake any foundation within minutes.'

Elizabeth grimaced. 'My skin isn't as young as yours, Caroline.'

'You're only six years older than I am, Elizabeth.'

'Six years!' The older woman wrinkled her nose. 'Darling, when you get to thirty, those six years can seem a lifetime.'

Elizabeth finally emerged, small and delicate, in the attractive green linen, making Caroline more than ever conscious of the disparities between them. She felt tall and ungainly, all arms and legs in her brief shirt and shorts, totally unaware that her body was smoothly rounded and that she possessed a natural elegance which Elizabeth could never hope to achieve. Even so, no one would have guessed that only fifteen minutes earlier Elizabeth had been morose and dishevelled, reluctant to even make the effort to dress. Now she positively sparkled, her smile well in evidence as she shook hands with her husband's employer and spoke affectionately to the children.

'Ask Thomas for some coffee, Caroline, will you?' she suggested, after the initial formalities were over, and Caroline made a casual movement of her head before going to do her bidding. She understood that Elizabeth wanted to speak to her visitor alone, and while Caroline was treated as an equal on most planes, this was one occasion when the other woman wanted to show her authority.

Thomas smiled his usual acquiescence, and then said: 'Mrs. Lacey not wanting shower now, miss?'

Caroline shook her head. 'No,' she agreed. 'Not now.'

Deciding to go back to her room to finish her packing, she was surprised a few minutes later when Miranda came looking for her.

'Mummy wants you, Caroline,' she said. 'Can you come?'

Caroline rose to her feet. 'I suppose so. Hasn't Thomas given them their coffee yet?'

'Oh, yes. But he brought three cups and Mr. Freeleng asked where you were.'

'Oh, I see.' Caroline digested this thoughtfully. 'All right, Miranda, I'll come.'

Back in the lounge, Nicolas rose to his feet politely at her entrance, but Elizabeth looked rather put out. After handing Caroline a cup of coffee, she said: 'Mr. Free-leng——'

'—Nicolas, please.'

'Yes.' Elizabeth forced a smile. 'Well, Nicolas—has invited us to dine with him this evening, and I've been trying to explain that naturally you will stay here and look after the children. Isn't that right?'

Caroline seated herself on the edge of a chair, and Nicolas resumed his position on the couch. 'Of course,' she nodded, and sipped her coffee.

'Mr. Freeleng said that if Caroline didn't come to dine because of us then we could go, too,' asserted David with his usual lack of tact. 'Can we, Mummy, can we?'

Elizabeth turned cold eyes in Caroline's direction. 'I imagine Mr. Free—Nicolas, that is, was only being polite.'

'On the contrary.' Now it was Nicolas's turn. 'My invitation includes all of you. Surely it's inconceivable to expect Miss Ashford to refuse all invitations while she's here in order to take care of David and Miranda? I'm quite sure a more satisfactory arrangement could be reached. I've no doubt that Thomas would be prepared——'

'I do not intend to leave my children in the charge of a—a houseboy!' Elizabeth sounded annoyed now.

'Why not?' David protested. 'It would be great. He probably knows all about witchcraft and black magic and that sort of thing! He might even know of some head-hunters——'

'That will do, David!' Elizabeth's temper was definitely rising.

Nicolas shrugged. 'Very well then, if you would prefer a European to stay with the children, I suggest you allow me to contact Lucas Macdonald. He's the physician in charge of the men's health at the mine, and his daughter, Sandra, I'm sure would be delighted to come here this evening and sit with them.'

In the silence that followed this statement they all heard the sound of a car drawing up outside and presently the door of the bungalow opened and Charles came into the room.

'Well, hello, Nick,' he greeted the other man cheerfully. 'I thought I recognised that automatic monster outside.' He bent to kiss his wife's cheek, and Caroline could sense from her withdrawal that he was instantly made aware that something was wrong. 'What's going on?'

Nicolas rose to his feet. 'I've just been issuing your wife with an invitation for you all to dine with me this evening. I've invited one or two people. I thought it would serve as a kind of welcome reception for Mrs. Lacey.'

'That sounds marvellous.' Charles glanced down at his

wife again. 'What do you think, Elizabeth?'

Before Elizabeth could make any comment, however, Nicolas went on: 'Unfortunately, there seems to be some difficulty about Miss Ashford being able to join us. Your wife is concerned about the children being left with Thomas——'

Charles drew out his cigarettes and offered them around. 'I see.'

Elizabeth looked up at him impatiently. 'I've been explaining that the reason Caroline came out here with us was to look after the children!' she said coldly.

Caroline thrust down her cup and rose also. 'I'm quite prepared to do it,' she cried. 'I don't mind——'

'Oh, nonsense!' Charles apparently agreed with Nicolas Freeleng in this. 'If Nicolas has invited you, too, then of course you must go.'

Nicolas's face mirrored his satisfaction. 'So! I have suggested that Sandra Macdonald might be prepared to sit with the children this evening.'

'Of course. Sandra!' Charles's expression cleared. 'Yes, she'd do it. Darling,' he turned to his wife, 'that's a good idea. Sandra is completely trustworthy and capable. She lives with her father only a few yards along from us. Her mother is dead, and she's become his housekeeper. She's a charming girl. How old would you say she was, Nick? Twenty-five—twenty-six?'

'Something like that,' agreed Nicolas, nodding. 'So—shall I contact her or will you?'

'I'll arrange it.' Charles was trying to ignore his wife's ungraciousness. 'Now, can I offer you a drink, Nick? Coffee's okay, but I'm ready for something a bit more thirst-quenching.'

But Nicolas shook his head. 'I'm afraid I can't stay, Charles, my friend. I have other calls to make.' He turned to Elizabeth and took her hand. 'Goodbye until this evening, Mrs. Lacey. I hope you will forgive me for overruling your wishes, but I can assure you, any anxiety so far as the children is concerned is quite unnecessary. They'll be in safe hands.'

Elizabeth forced a smile. 'Till this evening, Mr.—I mean —Nicolas.'

Nicolas turned to Caroline. 'So you are to join us after all,' he said, and only she could see the imp of mischief in his dark eyes. 'I'll look forward to it.'

Charles went with his employer to the door, and Caroline hesitated only a moment before gathering together the coffee cups and putting them on the tray. She dared hardly look at Elizabeth, and was not surprised when she ordered the children to their rooms to wash their hands before lunch. Then she said:

'Well, I must say you're a cool one!'

Caroline sighed and straightened, looking at the other woman resignedly. 'Elizabeth, it wasn't my idea.'

'No, but you didn't protest overmuch, did you? You left it all to me. I felt like some—some Victorian matriarch forbidding a servant to take a well-earned night off!'

'Oh, Elizabeth!'

'And when David said that you had suggested taking them along as well——'

'I didn't suggest that!' exclaimed Caroline indignantly. 'Nicolas Freeleng did!'

'Oh, really?' Elizabeth looked sceptical. 'And are you trying to tell me that in the space of the few minutes it would take for you to let him in and find out what he wanted he took such a liking to you that he insisted that you come whatever the outcome?'

'I didn't *let* him in,' retorted Caroline impatiently. 'He came in *with* me. We met him on our walk, and he gave us

51

a lift back.'

'What?' Elizabeth stared at her in amazement. 'You mean he picked you up?'

'Not like that, no.' Caroline was looking terribly embarrassed when Charles came back into the room, rubbing his hands.

'Well, that's settled, then,' he remarked cheerfully, evidently hoping that his wife would have accepted the situation by now. 'I'll have a word with Sandra this afternoon.'

Elizabeth rose to her feet. 'And if I refuse?'

'What do you mean?' Charles sounded weary.

'If I refuse to let this strange woman look after David and Miranda, what then?'

'Then you'll be obliged to stay at home and look after them yourself, won't you?' remarked her husband mildly, and left the room before she could say anything else.

Sandra Macdonald turned out to be an attractive, cheerful young woman, with a smooth cap of nut-brown hair and a comfortably curved figure. Although Caroline herself had little to do with her before they left she was relieved to see that Sandra seemed to laugh a lot and the children were taking to her. She and her father arrived at Charles's instigation about half an hour before they were due to leave for Nicolas Freeleng's dinner party and he served them drinks while Elizabeth finished dressing.

Caroline had chosen to wear a simple turquoise hostess gown. Made of a synthetic fibre, it had a low rounded neckline, and long sleeves, while the long skirt accentuated the rounded outline of her hips. When she joined Charles and the Macdonalds in the lounge before leaving she felt absurdly self-conscious, and wished she had insisted on remaining behind with the children. What must these people think of a nursemaid who went out to dine with her employer and his wife?

52

Fortunately, the conversation had not progressed beyond the vagaries of the British weather before Elizabeth joined them, and they all walked out to the car together. Lucas Macdonald took his leave, promising to call in again within the next few days, and Elizabeth issued Sandra with some final instructions before getting into the car beside her husband. Although David and Miranda had already been put to bed, Caroline saw two small shadowy figures in the recesses of the hall, watching them as they drove away.

It seemed to be taking them some time to reach Nicolas Freeleng's house and when the lights of the settlement at La Vache disappeared behind a belt of tropical forest, Caroline couldn't help leaning forward and saying: 'Exactly where are we going?'

Charles glanced back over his shoulder and smiled at her. 'Oh, Nick lives at Nyshasa, Caroline. Didn't I tell you? Wait until you see his house. It's quite something, believe me!'

Caroline sank back against the cool upholstery. After the heat of the day it was very refreshing to feel anything cold against her warm flesh. But the heat that was spreading through her now had nothing to do with the climate. Gareth lived at Nyshasa, too. He had said so.

A surge of excitement ran through her. All day she had kept thoughts of Gareth at bay, but now they would not be denied. She had tried not to speculate on how she was going to contrive to see him again, but perhaps it was not going to be as difficult as she had imagined.

They reached Nyshasa by crossing a high, precariously-balanced bridge over some falls which in daylight Charles assured them were spectacularly beautiful.

'As soon as I have some free time we'll bring a picnic up here,' he said. 'The kids would like that, and you can bathe in the water. It's swift-running and clear, and quite free of infection.'

The sound of the falls was still in their ears as they turned from the narrow bridge along a track that seemed to skirt the tumbling river. Low, overhanging branches touched the roof of the car as Charles steered it slowly along the precipitous edge of a ravine, and then, much to everyone's relief, the track wound upward between the trees and they saw ahead of them the lights of a house.

'This is it,' remarked Charles, as the bushes swept aside to reveal a clearing where a white-painted, two-storied dwelling shed artificial illumination over a gravelled fore-court. The sound of music and voices echoed from the verandah where Nicolas and his other guests were already enjoying drinks, and Charles parked his station wagon behind a dusty Landrover.

Behind and above the building, the thickly foliaged side of the ravine mounted to a velvety skyline, and in daylight the view from the windows at the front of the house must be quite magnificent, thought Caroline, as she climbed, un-aided, out of the back of the car.

Elizabeth's mutual admiration of Nicolas Freeleng's house banished any trace of tension between them, and when Nicolas himself came down the shallow steps to greet them, Elizabeth became the charming young woman Charles Lacey had first fallen in love with.

'I'm so glad you could come,' enthused their host, en-compassing them all in that instantaneous welcome. 'Come along and meet my guests. Charles knows them already, of course.'

Caroline followed Elizabeth and Nicolas up the steps to the verandah with Charles at her side. She was glad of the shadowy darkness to hide her own nervousness, but the light there was had been sufficient for her to distinguish the silver-flecked fairness of a tall man's hair.

CHAPTER FOUR

THE meal, which was served in an attractive dining-room at the back of the house, was excellent by any standards, and certainly Elizabeth could have nothing to complain about with regard to the ability of Nicolas Freeleng's chef. An iced consommé of veal was followed by fried chicken and rice, and a crisp salad, and there was a strawberry mousse for dessert which melted in the mouth. The house-boys also saw to it that no one's wine glass remained empty for very long, and Caroline found herself covering her glass with her palm and shaking her head apologetically as they passed. She wasn't used to drinking wine after a liberal spate of Martinis, and she had no desire to become intoxicated and make a fool of herself. Particularly not with Gareth Morgan there to witness her every move.

Since their arrival and the perfunctory greetings which had been exchanged, she had not spoken to him. But as Nicolas appeared to have made himself her escort for the evening, perhaps that was not so surprising. All the same, her eyes had been drawn to the attractive appearance he presented in a dark lounge suit, his sun-bleached hair a startling contrast to the darkness of his tan. He was obviously quite at home in Nicolas's house, and had been roped in as a kind of bar steward before dinner, serving drinks from the trolley the houseboy had wheeled on to the verandah.

As well as Caroline, Gareth and the Laceys, Nicolas had invited his mine superintendent and his wife, and an un-attached young South African who was, Nicolas explained, in the process of doing a survey on mine management.

Julian Holland, the mine superintendent, was a man in his fifties, with iron-grey hair and a spare, slightly stooping frame. His wife, Joan, was of a similar age, but she was small and plump, with hair that she apparently permed herself and a brown, weathered complexion. She was the kind of female Caroline had expected to find in an outpost like this—friendly, but inquisitive, her only real enjoyment being derived from the kind of gossip practised over the coffee cups everywhere.

During the meal, the conversation veered inevitably towards masculine topics, and Caroline amused herself between courses by examining the attractive accoutrements of the room. The house was built of logs, somewhat like a ranch-house, and no attempt had been made to disguise the fact. On the contrary, the rough walls formed an ideal background for the hunting trophies which adorned them, while an enormous fireplace looked big enough to roast some of the smaller species of game. The polished floor was strewn with skin rugs, and there were rifles in a kind of rack by the door. The sight of the weapons caused Caroline no small sense of unease, and yet in wild surroundings like these one had to be prepared for every eventuality.

When the meal was over, they all adjourned to a comfortable lounge where a log fire was leaping up the chimney. Caroline thought it was an unnecessary addition to an already warm room, but the sight of the flames was cheering, as it was intended to be.

Having gauged Elizabeth's reasons for being in Africa from her before the meal, when it was over Joan Holland sought Caroline's company. Caroline had seated herself on a low couch some distance from the fireplace and was presently trying to concentrate on Elizabeth helping Nicolas to serve coffee and liqueurs when all the while she was intensely conscious of Gareth standing just inside the door,

56

talking to Charles and possibly deciding where to sit. Her nails were curled tightly into her palms and she was stiff with tension when the gossipy little woman subsided on to the couch beside her.

'Do you mind if I sit here?' she enquired, unnecessarily, clearly not prepared for a refusal, and when Caroline shook her head, trying to contain her disappointment, she went on: 'And how are you settling down here? Do you find the heat trying?'

Caroline shook her head again. 'Not really,' she answered shortly, but Joan Holland was not to be deterred.

'Mrs. Lacey tells me you're a school teacher,' she remarked. 'Is that right?'

Caroline nodded. 'That is my profession,' she agreed.

'And you could leave it to come out here and act as a kind of nanny to Mrs. Lacey's children?'

Caroline smoothed the folds of her dress. 'It makes a change to have a break now and then,' she answered quietly.

'I'm sure it does. But I'm surprised you're not afraid your place will have been filled by the time you get back.'

'I've no doubt my place will have been filled, but there's quite a demand for teaching staff in England,' Caroline returned dryly.

'Really?' Her companion accepted a cup of coffee from the tray the houseboy proffered and added two spoonfuls of sugar. 'You'll find life out here vastly different from what you've been used to, you know. It's not the romantic wilderness that novelists make it out to be. We don't have any entertainment—any social life except what we make for ourselves. There are no theatres or dance-halls here, Miss Ashford.'

'I've never particularly sought that kind of entertainment, Mrs. Holland,' retorted Caroline, resenting the implied criticism in the other woman's voice. 'And I quite expect to find life very different.'

Joan Holland's eyebrows ascended at this, and she cast a comprehensive glance around the room as though to assure herself that she was not missing anything before continuing: 'Julian and I have been in Africa for more than twenty years. Not permanently in Tsaba, of course. Julian's worked in Rhodesia and South Africa, and his last appointment was in Zambia.'

Caroline forced an attentiveness she did not feel. She sipped her coffee and wished she had not evaded Nicolas's suggestion that she should help him serve the coffee and liqueurs. How foolish she had been to expect that Gareth might make any move towards her simply because she was sitting alone!

'I think Julian wants to speak to you, Joan.'

The clipped male tones halted the older woman in full spiel, and Caroline's nerve-ends tingled as she looked up into Gareth Morgan's lean face.

Joan Holland drained her coffee cup before replying: 'Julian wants to speak to me, Gareth?' She frowned. 'Do you know why?' Her eyes were on her husband as she spoke, and looking across the room Caroline could see that he was absorbed in conversation with Jonas Berg, the young South African student, and seemed totally unconcerned as to his wife's whereabouts.

'I think he said something about losing his spectacles,' remarked Gareth easily, his thumbs hooked into the low belt of his trousers. 'Why don't you go and find out?'

Joan glared searchingly into his tanned face and then cast a speculative look at Caroline. Getting reluctantly to her feet, she brushed down her skirt and said: 'Oh, well, if he wants me, I'd better go and see why, hadn't I?'

Gareth allowed a faint smile of assent to touch the corners of his mouth. Joan gave him another piercing stare and then marched irritably away. Gareth half turned to watch her progress and then, much to Caroline's astonishment, lowered his weight on to the couch beside her.

For a few awkward seconds Caroline could think of nothing to say, but then the inevitable question sprang to her lips: 'Did Mr. Holland really want to speak to his wife?' The words came out with a breathless little emphasis, but she had turned to look at him as she spoke and she was intensely aware of his thigh only inches away from hers on the soft skin covering of the couch. Relaxed beside her, he was even more disturbingly attractive than she remembered, and the desire to make him aware of her as she was of him was of paramount importance.

He returned her gaze with cool analysis and it took all her will power not to succumb to the urge to lower her lids before that detached appraisal. 'Not as far as I know,' he conceded dryly.

'Then—then why did you——' She broke off uncertainly, aware of a sudden flickering of something rather unpleasant in the blue depths confronting her.

'Why did I what?' he enquired coldly. 'Interrupt your tête-à-tête with Mrs. Holland?' He shrugged. 'I felt sorry for you, although why I should I can't imagine. But no one cares for Joan's unsubtle inquisitions.'

'I see.' Caroline's spirits sank, and now she did avert her eyes. 'So it wasn't done to enable you to speak to me.'

Gareth considered her downbent head. 'And what do you suppose I might have to say to you?' he enquired dispassionately.

Caroline moved her shoulders, irritation vying with discretion. 'Don't you think this is all rather ridiculous, Gareth?' she demanded in a low voice. 'We're adult human beings. Whatever happened all those years ago is gone and

—and forgotten. I wish you would stop behaving as if we were antagonists!'

Gareth drew out a case of cigars and placed one between even white teeth before replying. As he searched for his lighter, he said: 'But I do feel antagonistic towards you, Caroline, and I see no reason to pretend otherwise. If you want me to be brutally honest then I'll tell you that I think you have a bloody nerve coming out here!'

This devastating denunciation was delivered in a calm, unemotional tone, and no one watching him or even hearing the murmur of his voice could have divined from his manner exactly what he was saying. But Caroline could hear, only too well, and anger dispelled any lingering trace of nervousness.

'I think you're behaving like a boor,' she accused, fighting against the desire for her voice to rise. 'I don't honestly see why you have to feel antagonistic towards me. Our relationship was hardly a permanent one when within a year of our—our separation you married someone else!'

She had neither meant nor wanted to bring up the question of his previous marriage, and now that she had she wished impotently that she hadn't. Her words hung between them, a tangible presence in the air, chilling the heated atmosphere.

'I do not intend to discuss the subject of my marriage with you, Caroline,' said Gareth at last. 'Indeed, I would prefer it if we didn't talk at all.'

'Don't you think that would look rather obvious?' she enquired, hiding her feelings in an attempt at sarcasm. 'Particularly as Mrs. Holland has hardly taken her eyes off us since she got up out of that seat!'

Gareth's lips curved, but only Caroline knew that his smile did not reach his eyes. 'I don't particularly care what Mrs. Holland thinks,' he remarked unpleasantly. 'But if you want to keep up the pretence of casual acquaintances exchanging small talk, then go ahead.'

Caroline clenched his fists. 'You're really trying to hurt me, aren't you, Gareth? I wonder why? Could it be that you don't find me quite as repulsive as you'd like?'

She didn't know what made her say that. Certainly she never for one moment believed it. But the reaction it stimulated startled her. His hand moved with rapier-like swiftness across the space between them, imprisoning her wrist in a grip so painfully tight that she saw the blood receding rapidly. She cast a horrified glance around the room, but no one had noticed their small contretemps. Only a moment before, Mrs. Holland had been diverted from her embarrassing observation by Charles drawing her attention to a rather attractive watercolour hanging above the fireplace, and as everyone else was occupied Gareth's action had gone unobserved. She would have liked to have tried to free herself, but that would surely have been noticed, and in any case Gareth was pretending to look at her wristwatch.

'I don't intend to warn you again, Caroline,' he muttered, grimly. 'Keep away from me!'

Her eyes sought his. 'And if I don't?'

'Then I won't be responsible for the consequences.'

'I don't know what you mean.'

'Oh, yes, you do, Caroline.' His eyes were hard and distrustful. 'You played me for a fool seven years ago. Well, maybe that was partially my fault. I should have had more sense than to get involved with an immature schoolgirl——'

'I was young, I admit that. But what we shared was good, Gareth,' she protested, trying to draw her hand away. 'Please let me go. You're hurting me!'

'Hurting you?' He surveyed her scornfully. 'I could hurt you a damn sight more than this, believe me.' He flung her wrist back into her lap and she rubbed the stinging flesh, realising she was going to have quite a bruise by the next day. 'You won't make a fool of me a second time, Caroline. It may be a painful process, but one learns by one's mistakes.'

Caroline put a protective hand over her reddening wrist. Perhaps she deserved that. After all, she had been responsible for their break-up. She could still remember the blazing row they had had the night she told him she couldn't marry him. But that was in the past again. She forced her thoughts back to the immediate present.

'So it's no use my saying I'm sorry,' she ventured quietly.

'You're sorry!' He stared at her with an incredulous mixture of anger and derision. 'My God, Caroline, that beats all!'

'Why? Why shouldn't I say I'm sorry? I am. Very.'

'I'll bet you are!' He stared at her for another long moment and then shook his head disbelievingly. 'Oh, Caroline, what an admission! I've heard everything now. What's brought this on? Have you just begun to realise that you're not a teenager any longer, and that that comfortable meal-ticket for life is passing you by? What happened to all those high ideals? Things must be rough if you've had to resort to this!'

His words were the cruellest she had ever heard. They bit deeply into her heart, taking a stranglehold on her emotions. She badly wanted to hurt him then. She would have liked to have struck him, slapped that sardonic contempt from his lean face, battered at him with her fists until he begged for mercy. But of course, even without the paralysing associations of their surroundings, she could never do that. He was too powerful, too strong for her ever to physically damage him. With one hand he had once been able to imprison both of hers behind her back, propelling her towards him, feeding from her mouth with a hunger which only she had been capable of assuaging. And during this time she had been attending a sixth form college, working for her 'A' levels, listening to other girls giggling about the boys they had dated the night before. She had never indulged in that kind of childishness, in fact she had gained a reputation for being aloof; but no one had suspected that the man who sometimes picked her up at the college gates in his sleek Rover saloon was anything other than the uncle she pretended him to be. Looking back on it now, she wondered whether circumstances had not had some bearing on her decision. Maybe if she had been able to discuss her feelings with someone other than her mother who had been biased from the start she would not have made such a terrible mistake.

She suddenly realised that Gareth was still watching her, and with a muffled exclamation she rose to her feet. But to her surprise he rose too, looking down at her with a strange expression in his eyes.

'Are you all right?' he asked in a low voice, and she realised with a fleeting sense of despair that he was concerned about her. Basically, he was a decent man—wasn't that one of the reasons she had fallen in love with him, why she still loved him?—and although he despised her as a woman, he could still feel concern for her as a fellow human being. Or was she perhaps being too charitable? Maybe it was simply that he was afraid of what she might betray to the others in this distressed state. She felt suddenly cold. Was that all that was left for her in him? An impersonal regard to her physical condition?

'Oh, Gareth,' she breathed, raising tear-filled eyes to his face, and his expression hardened into resignation.

'At last,' he commented dryly. 'The ultimate weapon—tears! Dear me, Caroline, you'll have to do better than that!'

She caught her breath at his callousness, and the tears

froze behind her eyes. How could he? she thought, a violent hatred against him flooding her being where before there had been weakness and regret. She itched to rake her nails down his sarcastic cheek. How dared he speak to her in such a way? Oh, why had she ever imagined that time might have healed the gulf between them? All she had done was lay herself open to ridicule and humiliation. A desire to make him suffer as he was making her suffer was conceived inside her, and she started violently when a casual voice said:

'Come on, Gareth! You can't monopolise the lady all evening!'

While Caroline endeavoured to gather her composure, Gareth turned to his friend with infuriating coolness. 'I'm sorry, Nick,' he apologised. 'Was I doing that?' He allowed his mocking gaze to flicker with casual insolence over Caroline. 'I must have forgotten the time. You know how it is.'

Caroline felt tension like a ball inside her, but two could play at that game, she thought, with unaccustomed maliciousness.

'Yes, it's always—*fun*—to talk over old times, isn't it, Garry?' she agreed sweetly, knowing how much he detested the diminutive form of his name. 'You must forgive us, Mr. Freeleng.'

Nicolas laughed and assured her that she made him feel quite old when she insisted on addressing him so formally, but even as he spoke she was conscious of Gareth's surprised stiffening beside her. She was inordinately glad. No doubt he had thought her completely shattered by the events of the past few minutes, but if she was, she had no intention of letting him see. There was more than one way to win a war, she was beginning to realise, and perhaps all the weapons were not on his side after all.

'I expect you two do find things to talk about,' Nicolas was saying now. 'You used to live near Gareth's sister, I understand, Caroline.'

'Yes, that's right. But after my mother died, I moved away.'

Nicolas nodded, then he grinned at the other man. 'Still, Gareth, you mustn't keep it all to yourself, you know. She wasn't brought along here for your benefit.'

Gareth half smiled, a rather unpleasant little smile, Caroline thought. Then he said: 'I know she wasn't, Nick. To be quite honest, I was—surprised she came.'

'Why?' Nicolas raised his dark brows.

'Well, I understood she came out here to take care of Lacey's children.' A sidelong glance was intended to be demoralising, and Caroline's temper simmered. 'I was sure she'd be roped in to babysit.'

Caroline longed to say something devastating, but of course she couldn't. It was left to Nicolas to explain, but she had the sense to realise that Gareth was telling her in no uncertain terms that he had not come here this evening expecting to see her.

'You're not sugesting that a delicious morsel like this should be left to play nursemaid, when someone else is quite prepared to take over, are you, Gareth?'

Gareth shrugged. 'Someone has to do it.'

'Agreed. And Mac's daughter was more than willing.' Nicolas's smile widened. 'Now, tell me, don't you think that suits her talents more admirably than Caroline's?'

Caroline's face burned. They were talking about her as if she wasn't present, and while she understood that Nicolas meant no harm, she could not be so sure of Gareth.

He straightened from pressing out his cigar in an ashtray and answered: 'You could be right. Sandra certainly does have a way with children—with anyone.'

'Including you, my friend,' Nicolas chuckled, and turned to Caroline. 'You must forgive me, but I think Gareth has quite a soft spot for Sandra, and it's certain that she has a soft spot for him!'

Caroline's answering smile was a little set. 'Really?'

'I'm afraid so.' Nicolas shook his head. 'She's been a great comfort to him recently, hasn't she, Gareth?'

Gareth made a casual movement of his shoulders. 'If it pleases you to think so, Nick.'

Nicolas nodded. 'Yes—well, I get the impression that that subject is taboo, so let me get you a drink, Caroline, and you can tell me what you think of my house.'

For the remainder of the evening Nicolas never strayed far from her side. After the coffee cups were cleared away and more drinks were served, the record player was set in motion, and the younger members of the party danced. Once while she was drifting round the floor in Nicolas's arms, Caroline saw Mrs. Holland take up a position beside Gareth, and she wondered what explanation if any he offered for his tardy dismissal of her earlier in the evening. He himself made no attempt to dance with anyone, and although she would have loved to have gone across and asked him it was too soon to attempt to put any kind of plan into action. Nicolas's words about Sandra Macdonald had shaken her somewhat. Until that moment the fact that Gareth was no longer married had meant to her that he was free. But what if his marriage had failed because of his involvement with someone else? Someone like Sandra Macdonald, for example. It was quite a thought.

Nicolas, of course, was charming and amusing, and she found herself liking him more and more. It was good to know that at least one person present had sought her company, and every time they passed the couch where Gareth was sitting, she became deliberately attentive to her partner, ignoring the contemptuous curve of Gareth's mouth as he watched them. She drank more than she had done before, too, but the alcohol helped enormously in dulling her pained senses, and the determination to make Gareth pay for his cruelty was still strong in her mind when Charles drove them home just after eleven.

She slept that night the minute her head touched the pillow, and it was not until the next morning that a blinding headache reminded her of everything that had happened.

CHAPTER FIVE

DAVID and Miranda were full of enthusiasm for Sandra Macdonald. Apparently she had read them a story the previous evening before settling them down for sleep, and had told them that if they were good they could go to tea at her house the next afternoon.

'She said that there are twins living next door to her,' added David excitedly. 'They're boys and they're only six years old. Sandra said that when they're eight they'll go to school in England, but for the moment she's teaching them.'

'Is she?' Caroline tried to sound interested, but the aspirins she had taken seemed to be making not the slightest impression on her headache.

'Yes,' answered Miranda, nodding. 'Their names are John and Joseph, and their mummy and daddy come from South Africa.'

'Really?' Caroline forced a smile, gathering together their breakfast dishes for Thomas. Elizabeth had not joined them this morning and as yet Caroline had not attempted to disturb her. Charles had left for the mine earlier, of course, but the children's mother was obviously tired after their night out.

When breakfast was cleared away, David and Miranda asked whether they might take a ball into the back garden. This was the stretch of scrub at the back of the bungalow and after consulting with Thomas, Caroline could see no reason why not. She herself had some washing to do, and Thomas agreed to heat some water for her.

It wasn't good working in the heat with a headache, and

by the time her and the children's underclothes had been washed and draped over an outside line to dry in the sun she was feeling quite sick. She was in the kitchen, breaking ice cubes out of the container for a cool drink, when a car pulled up outside. She wiped her hand and walked into the hall just as their visitor reached the mesh door and she saw to her astonishment that it was Gareth. When he saw her he opened the door and came striding down the hall towards her, while she backed into the kitchen, overwhelmingly conscious of her shabby jeans and navy cotton vest.

'What in God's name have you been doing?' he demanded harshly, taking the glass from her and tackling the ice cubes himself. 'Where's Thomas?'

Caroline shook her head, wiping the back of her hand across her forehead. 'I'm not sure. Tidying up the living-room, probably.'

Gareth regarded her hot face. 'Where are the children?'

'They're playing outside. Look, let me do that.'

Gareth shook his head impatiently and after a few moments handed her back the glass, liberally filled with ice cubes, ready for her to pour in some freshly squeezed lemon juice.

'Will you have some?' she offered, prepared to divide the cubes, but he shook his head. Then she added: 'Elizabeth's still in bed, I think. She—she was tired after last night. Do—do you want to see her?' She couldn't imagine that he might want to see her, not after last night, and in her confused state of the moment she hadn't the strength to fence with him.

'What are you to her?' he bit out savagely, catching sight of the washing drying on the line. 'What does she pay you to perform such menial tasks?'

Caroline shook her head, trying not to look at him. His cream shirt was open at the throat exposing a brown column

69

of hair-roughened skin, glinting with gold, while his beige trousers were cut narrowly over his thighs, exposing the muscles of his legs, hard and taut beneath the fine cloth. After last night she should have been hating him, she knew, but the nausea she had been feeling had weakened her resolve and she longed to be able to touch him, to get close to him, if not physically then at least mentally.

At last she managed to say: 'What has that got to do with you? Shall I tell Elizabeth you're here?'

Gareth raked a hand through his hair, his action dragging her eyes to his face, and for a long moment she met his exasperated stare. Then he smote the ball of his fist against his thigh and said: 'If you like. I want her permission to take the children up to Nyshasa.'

Caroline's lips parted involuntarily. 'To—to Nyshasa?' she breathed. 'But you live at Nyshasa.'

'That's right,' Gareth nodded briefly, but Caroline's heart was pounding thunderously.

'Is—is that where you're taking them?' she asked faintly.

Gareth's eyes narrowed. 'That's right. I thought they might like to paddle in the river.'

Caroline pressed her palms together. 'Oh, I'm sure they'd love it,' she asserted, imagining the delight of submerging her overheated body in the cool waters of the falls. 'Will you give us a few minutes to get ready? Elizabeth won't object, I'm certain.'

Gareth's expression hardened. 'I'm sorry,' he said, and now his voice had perceptibly stiffened. 'I thought I made the invitation clear. It's for the children only.'

Caroline could feel the blood draining out of her cheeks, and she sought the edge of the refrigerator for support. Staring at him as if she couldn't believe her ears, she murmured: 'What?'

'You can have the day off,' remarked Gareth shortly.

'Sandra's waiting in the car. She can handle the children. She phoned me this morning and suggested the outing.'

He could not have dashed her hopes more brutally, and Caroline felt sick with reaction. He must have known that she would expect the invitation to include her and it had been just another exhibition of the ways he could hurt her.

She forced herself to move away from the refrigerator and said: 'I see. Well, just a minute and I'll speak to Elizabeth.'

Elizabeth was only half awake and perfectly willing to delegate her responsibilities to someone else. Fortunately, she was drowsy enough not to notice Caroline's strained manner, and after gaining her permission the younger girl quickly left the room.

All the same, it took every scrap of will power to force herself to re-enter the kitchen, but Gareth was not there. He was outside talking to the children, and when they glimpsed Caroline by the door, they came bounding across to her yelling: 'Can we go; can we, Caroline?'

Caroline nodded. 'Your mother has no objections.' She compelled herself to glance in Gareth's direction. 'When will you bring them back?'

'I don't know exactly.' Gareth thrust his hands deep into the pockets of his trousers. 'Some time after five, I should imagine. Will that do?'

'Perfectly.' Caroline turned aside and they followed her into the house. Fortunately the children had not been outside long enough to get dirty and the only instructions she had to issue were for them to go to their room and get their swimsuits out of the chest. While they were gone she shook out a couple of towels for them and Gareth walked lazily through to the lounge. She heard him speaking to Thomas and then he returned to stand silent and un-approachable by the door. Not that she wanted to approach

71

him, she told herself fiercely. All the same, the pain he had inflicted would not be denied, and she wished they would hurry up and leave so that she could release the tight band of tension that bound her.

At last the children returned, and Gareth urged them towards the door. 'G'bye, Caroline!' they chorused, and Caroline endeavoured to smile and wave them off. But although she waved at Sandra Macdonald, she could not force herself to go out to the station wagon and speak to her casually, as if nothing was wrong. On the contrary, she felt she could have scratched the other girl's eyes out, so envious did she feel, and she went back into the bungalow as they drove away, slamming the door childishly behind her.

Of course, she didn't need a crystal ball to know what was the matter with her. She was jealous, agonisingly jealous, and as she stared at her reflection in the pitted mirror above the wash-stand in her bedroom, she felt a surge of self-contempt. She must pull herself together. She wasn't naturally a vindictive girl, and she was allowing her feelings for Gareth to get out of all proportion. In the years of his marriage, she had had to accept the situation, so why not now?

The answer to that was that in those days Gareth had been thousands of miles away, out of reach and out of touch, his marriage an unreal and impersonal relationship. But now that she was here, now that she had seen him again and experienced that awful, wanton longing for him sweeping over her, everything had become sharp and acute. And to imagine him attracted to Sandra Macdonald, to think of him touching her—possibly even making love to her, drove all sane and sensible reasoning out of her mind ...

The following morning, Nicolas Freeleng appeared just as they were finishing breakfast. He breezed into the living-room cheerfully, bringing a definite lift to Caroline's spirits.

'Good morning, Caroline,' he greeted her. 'Good morning, kiddies! Where's your dear mama this morning?'

'Mummy doesn't usually get up for breakfast,' volunteered David at once. 'What's that under your arm?'

He pointed to a gun hanging loosely from Nicolas's shoulder, and Nicolas grinned: 'This, my young friend, is a rifle. Haven't you ever seen a rifle before?'

David was impressed, but Miranda shuddered, and said: 'Why have you brought it in here?'

'One doesn't leave guns lying about unattended in cars,' replied Nicolas amiably, then turned his attention to Caroline. 'You're looking rather depressed, pussycat. What's wrong? Had you begun to think I'd forgotten all about you?' he chuckled.

Caroline lifted the lid of the coffee pot. 'I hadn't given the matter a lot of thought,' she replied honestly. 'Would you like some coffee? There's plenty left.'

'I'd love some coffee,' accepted Nicolas, subsiding into the chair across the table from her, and draping his gun carefully over its back. 'Thomas! Another cup!'

The houseboy came in grinning amiably. ''Mornin', Massa Freeleng,' he greeted. 'You wantin' something to eat?'

'No, thank you, Thomas.' Nicolas shook his head. 'This will do fine.' After the houseboy had gone, he poured himself some coffee and then went on: 'I thought you all might like to come out with me today.'

Caroline looked at him in surprise, but David forestalled any comment she was about to make by boasting: 'We went out yesterday. To Nyshasa!'

Nicolas cast a look in his direction which would have

73

quelled a less confident mortal completely. 'I do know that. But Caroline didn't go with you, did she?'

'She wasn't asked.' David shrugged a little defensively. 'It wasn't my fault.'

'No one's suggesting it was,' exclaimed Caroline impatiently. Then to Nicolas: 'But how did you know?'

'I called on Gareth for a drink yesterday evening and he told me.'

'Oh, I see.' Caroline cupped her cheeks in her palms to hide their sudden flaming. She had thought Gareth had spent the evening at the Macdonalds'. Sandra had brought the children back herself at about six o'clock, but she had implied that Gareth was still at her house. Or had she? Caroline couldn't remember. Maybe it was simply a case of her believing what she thought to be the truth.

'So.' Nicolas finished his coffee and drew out his cigarettes. 'What about it? Or does the prospect of another swim in the river not appeal to you kids?'

Miranda's eyes sparkled. 'I want to come,' she cried. 'I wished Caroline had come with us yesterday.'

Caroline gave Nicolas a wry look, and his eyes twinkled. 'Well?' he urged. 'What about you?'

Caroline made a helpless gesture. 'I'd love to come, and perhaps Elizabeth would like to come, too.'

'Ah, well, I don't think so,' remarked Nicolas slowly. 'You see, I've taken the precaution of giving Charles the rest of the day off, and he'll be home soon to look after Elizabeth's welfare. He was quite agreeable to you and the children coming out with me.'

Caroline stared at him, unable to suppress a gasp of reluctant admiration for his impudence. 'You never expected us to refuse, did you?'

'Let's put it this way,' said Nicolas persuasively. 'I thought you wouldn't refuse to keep a lonely guy company,

74

not when you know how much he enjoys yours.'

Caroline shook her head. 'I don't know what to say.'

'Well, I do. Go get your swimsuits and meet me at the car.'

'I'll have to tell Elizabeth.'

'Very well. But be quick about it.'

Elizabeth blinked uncomprehendingly when Caroline explained that Charles had been given the rest of the day off. But she didn't look particularly pleased at the news that Caroline and the children were going out for the day with Nicolas Freeleng.

'But what do you know about him?' she protested, levering herself up on one elbow.

Caroline sighed. 'He's Charles's boss, and he's hardly likely to be planning an abduction scene with the children along, is he?'

Elizabeth had to concede that this was so, and as there were few further objections she could voice she had to let her go. Caroline sped to her room, stripped off her few garments and quickly donned a diminutive white bikini. Then she pulled on her jeans and vest again and snatched up a towel and her sunglasses. The prospect of the unexpected outing had banished her depression, and she refused to admit that part of her excitement stemmed from the knowledge that at Nyshasa there was always the possibility that she might see Gareth.

The perpendicular heights of the narrow bridge that spanned the River Kinzori at Nyshasa were spectacular in daylight. Below the somewhat swaying structure a tremendous volume of white-spumed water plunged down a rock cascade to be sucked greedily into a whirlpool at its base. Moss-covered rocks and huge feathery ferns fringed the falls, a continuance of the thickly matted undergrowth which grew with luxuriance down the sides of the ravine.

There was a dampness in the air, and the hysterical squawking of a flock of vividly coloured parakeets, disturbed by a marauding monkey, preceded their graceful flight into the air. Here the denseness, the intrusion of the jungle into any attempt at civilisation was evident, and anyone venturing far from the track would soon find themselves in difficulties.

They spent the morning some distance down-river from the falls and Caroline told herself she was glad. But Nicolas had explained that the construction of the Mburi dam, which Gareth was working on, was some distance upstream at the point where the Kinzori forked and consequently reduced its velocity. The dam was being built to harness all the waters of the Kinzori into generative power and eventually a hydro-electric plant was to be built near the falls.

At lunch time they went back to Nicolas's house where his houseboys had prepared a delicious meal of iced melon and chicken salad, followed by fresh fruit and coffee. David and Miranda were obviously tired after their energetic morning and were not at all averse to being led upstairs and left to sleep for a while in an attractive twin-bedded room under the eaves.

Downstairs, after ascertaining that Caroline wasn't at all sleepy, Nicolas put some records on the player and came to sit beside her on a comfortably cushioned lounger on the verandah. The view from this vantage point was, as Caroline had expected, quite magnificent, a sweeping greensward precipitating towards the turbulent waters of the Kinzori. There was no visible sign of any other habitation, although Nicolas told her that there was an African village set further downstream within sight of his house, but the somnolent buzz of the insects and the unhurried cry of the animals created the certain impression that one was alone in this green, isolated place.

A houseboy had placed a trolley containing bottles and glasses and a bucket of ice within his master's reach, and Nicolas poured Martinis and handed her one. Caroline took it reluctantly, determining not to overdo it this time, and tried not to feel too obviously embarrassed when he put his arm along the back of her seat.

'Tell me about yourself, Caroline,' he murmured, lightly stroking her hair with a lazy hand. 'Why haven't you been snapped up by some love-hungry male? I'm sure the men in England find you just as delectable as I do.'

Caroline smiled her acceptance of this pretty comment, but made no reply to it. Instead she traced the rim of her glass with her forefinger before asking: 'Where does Gareth Morgan live?'

Nicolas was taken aback by her question. He frowned, his eyes seeking answers in eyes now averted. 'Why do you ask? Do you intend to pay him a visit?' he queried.

Caroline shrugged. 'I was curious, that's all.'

'I see.' Nicolas raised his glass to his lips and took a mouthful of its contents. 'He lives at the site, of course. Where else would the resident civil engineer live?'

Caroline glanced at him out of the corners of her eyes. 'Of course. I wasn't thinking.'

Nicolas flicked a fly from the immaculate crease in his trousers. 'I've no doubt that a visit to the site could be arranged if you're interested. It's quite a construction they're building.'

'Thank you.' Caroline accepted his invitation half reluctantly. Her feelings about seeking Gareth out were divided. Although she didn't relish the prospect of further humiliation, nor could she contemplate the possibility of not seeing him again.

'I'll arrange it,' commented Nicolas dryly, and then returned to his intent scrutiny of her slightly pink cheeks.

'Do you mean to tell me there's no man back in England waiting impatiently for your return?'

Caroline sighed. 'Maybe there is,' she replied evasively. 'How long have you been in Tsaba, Mr. Freeleng?'

'Nicolas!' he insisted. Then: 'I suppose I've been here almost ten years. First in Ashenghi, and then at the mine.'

'But your real home isn't here, is it?'

'No. My family live in Johannesburg,' he agreed impatiently. 'Look, I don't want to talk about me. I'm very dull meat. I want to talk about you. Tell me all about yourself —where you live, your hobbies, your family.'

'I don't have any family,' said Caroline quietly.

'All right, then, tell me where you live. Gareth told me you trained to be a teacher.'

'Yes.' Caroline bent to place her glass on a glass-topped table beside her. She had not touched her drink and Nicolas gave her a wry look.

'What's wrong? Isn't it to your taste?'

'It's very nice, thank you. I—well, I'm just not used to drinking during the day.'

'One Martini isn't drinking,' Nicolas protested, and she had to smile. He sounded so put out at her refusal to accept his hospitality.

'This is a marvellous place!' she enthused, but Nicolas bent his head and touched his mouth to the warm skin of her upper arm.

'You're a temptress, do you know that?' he exclaimed, his arm about her closing on her shoulder. 'You're deliberately teasing me.'

'Oh, I'm not—really,' she gasped in alarm, suddenly aware of their extreme isolation here. She struggled to move out of his grasp. 'Isn't this a record of the Carpenters that's playing now? I adore their music, don't you——'

But Nicolas was not so easily diverted, and he was

drawing her back into the circle of his arms when a car came accelerating up the slope to the house. 'Blast!' he swore angrily, obviously annoyed at this unwelcome intrusion, but Caroline could not have been more relieved. Although her relief turned to something else when she encountered the grim face of the man who was just climbing out of his station wagon.

Nicolas had to release her then, and he rose to his feet and went down the shallow steps to greet the newcomer. 'Well, well, Gareth,' he said, walking towards him. 'You're an unexpected surprise!'

Gareth looked beyond Nicolas to Caroline and she sensed his awareness of her confusion as something like distaste flickered across his face. Then he looked at Nicolas. 'I was passing and I thought I'd call in for a drink,' he explained. 'However, if I'd known that you had—company——'

'—you'd have come anyway,' finished Nicolas, with a wry twist to his lips. He gestured towards the steps. 'You'd better come in now you're here. What'll you have? Something sharp and cool, or some beer?'

'Beer would suit me fine,' replied Gareth, stretching lazily, lean and disturbingly male in a cream shirt and shorts. 'Hello, Caroline. Fancy seeing you here!'

'Leave the girl alone,' commanded Nicolas goodnaturedly, his initial annoyance at Gareth's appearance disappearing beneath his genuine liking for the man. 'Excuse me a minute while I get the beer from the fridge, won't you?'

He went into the house and Caroline gave Gareth a slightly uneasy appraisal. 'Won't you sit down?' she suggested awkwardly, feeling at quite a disadvantage. 'It's very hot, isn't it?'

To her astonishment, Gareth walked the length of the verandah to relax beside her on the cushioned lounger, his

79

tanned legs stretched out in front of him. Then he looked sideways at her and she saw his eyes were not relaxed at all. 'Don't make small talk with me,' he advised sharply. 'What the hell are you doing here?'

Caroline might have expected him to make some comment on her presence at Nicolas's house, but what she was not prepared for was the anger in his tones. What was it to do with him what she did? She'd have thought he'd be only too glad to shift her company on to another man's shoulders in the circumstances. Unless ... Unless he was jealous! She savoured the idea. Was it possible?

She slanted a glance in his direction. 'I didn't think you'd care what I did,' she murmured provocatively.

'I don't,' he returned killingly. 'I only care about Nicolas.'

Caroline stifled the desire to retaliate in kind. She hadn't his command of language, and she was quite aware of her limitations when it came to verbal conflict. Forcing a faint smile to her lips, she said: 'Don't you think Nicolas is old enough to look after himself?'

Gareth's smile was not pleasant in return. 'Oh, yes, he can look after himself. Unfortunately, he sometimes requires a little encouragement to remain faithful to his wife!'

Caroline's lips parted in horror. 'He's married!' she breathed disbelievingly.

'And of course you didn't know.'

'No!' Caroline sat up stiffly. 'How could I? I'm not a mind-reader, and I can assure you Nicolas didn't tell me.'

Gareth studied her indignant face. 'What about Lacey? Didn't he say anything?'

'I haven't discussed Nicolas with Charles, if that's what you mean. There was no need. Until today I doubt whether Charles ever considered it necessary that I should be told such a thing.'

Gareth removed his disturbing gaze. 'You might be telling the truth,' he commented consideringly, making Caroline seethe with righteous anger. 'If you are it's good that I happened along.'

'And did you?'

'What?'

'Just—happen along?' Caroline's voice was cold.

'No. I knew you were here.'

'How did you know that?'

Gareth gave her a sideways glance. 'Does it matter?' His eyes were unwavering. 'Where are the kids?'

'Resting.' Caroline bent her head, unknowingly exposing the soft nape of her neck. 'So you see, there was no great seduction scene going on.'

'Now then—here we are!'

Nicolas came bustling cheerfully out of the house carrying several cans of beer, his eyes flickering instantly to where Gareth was seated beside Caroline. Caroline supposed that to an onlooker, unaware of what was being said, they must appear to be getting along famously, and she was tempted to imply just that. After all, Nicolas deserved some kind of a let-down after the way he had deliberately deceived her. He must have known that she knew nothing about his wife. He might even have children of his own. The realisation was humiliating.

Now Nicolas ripped off an automatic can-opener and poured its contents into a glass frosted with ice. Then he came along the verandah and handed the glass to Gareth. 'I think you'll find that to your liking, my friend.'

'Thanks,' Gareth nodded, but made no attempt to get up and allow Nicolas to resume his previous position. Instead, Nicolas had to draw up another chair and sit in it.

Conversation was somewhat stilted. It was as though they were all absorbed with their own thoughts, and Caroline thought she could guess what they were. Nicolas had to be wondering whether Gareth had said anything to her regarding his marriage, Gareth was no doubt contemptuous of the whole situation, while she knew that Nicolas was no longer to be trusted. It did not make for an easy relationship, and she was almost relieved when David and Miranda came scampering out to join them, flushed and bright-eyed after their sleep. David was delighted to see Gareth and lost no time in demanding to know when he was going to take them to see the hippos as he had promised. Miranda pretended to want to know, too, but Caroline sensed that her enthusiasm was diluted by no small trace of apprehension.

While Gareth spoke with the children, Caroline was aware of Nicolas's eyes on her, willing her to make some move so that he could speak to her alone. But she refused to meet his gaze. She could not forgive him for placing her in such an ambiguous position.

At last Gareth rose to go and Nicolas rose, too. He thrust his hands deep into his trousers' pockets and said: 'You're not by any chance going down to La Vache, are you, Gareth?'

Gareth turned to him, his eyes narrowed. 'As a matter of fact I am. Why?'

Nicolas shrugged. 'I wondered whether you might take the children home. I—er—I'm having a little dinner party this evening, and I thought perhaps Caroline might stay——'

'No, thank you.' Caroline spoke without waiting for him to finish what he had been about to say. 'I couldn't possibly do that. And—and as—Gareth—is going down to La Vache, perhaps he wouldn't mind taking all of us home. It—it would save you the journey, Nicolas.'

Nicolas looked furious at this summary dismissal of his plans. 'I wouldn't dream of it,' he stated sharply. 'I brought you here. Naturally I shall take you back.'

'But that's ridiculous, Nick,' declared Gareth, strolling lazily along the verandah and down the shallow steps. 'There's absolutely no reason why you should make a special journey when I'm going that way in any case.'

Put like that there was little more Nicolas could add. Without Caroline's support he was defeated, but she glimpsed the anger burning in his eyes. But her relief at escaping from an impossible situation was such that it was not until they were actually on their way to La Vache that she had pause to wonder whether her action might not reflect on Charles. But surely not. Nicolas couldn't be so vindictive, could he? And besides, what had she done after all?

Her anxiety communicated itself to Gareth and he gave her a swift look before picking up speed again as the bridge disappeared behind them. 'What's wrong?' he queried mockingly. 'Regretting it so soon?'

'You would think that, wouldn't you?' she countered, torturing the strap of her shoulder bag. 'As a matter of fact I was wondering whether—well, whether my coming away like this has made Nicolas very angry. I mean, angry enough to—to bear a grudge.'

'Against whom? You? I hardly think so.'

'No. I meant Charles, actually.'

'Charles.' Gareth's lips curled. 'Ah, is that to be your excuse? You'll only accept Nick's invitations to protect Charles! Now why didn't I think of that?'

Caroline bore his mockery in silence, hating the way he took every opportunity to make a fool of her. Why couldn't they ever have a normal conversation? If he really despised her so much why didn't he treat her with indifference and not with this almost cruel derision? Or did he simply get a certain amount of satisfaction out of hurting her?

Wanting to destroy his cool sarcasm, she said: 'And what will you do, Gareth? If I decide to go on meeting Nicolas?'

'I shouldn't have thought after the way you cut and run just now that there was much likelihood of that,' he replied.

'Wouldn't you?' Caroline assumed a nonchalance she was far from feeling, but a need for retaliation had convinced her that she might just as well be hanged for a sheep as a lamb. 'Well, perhaps you're taking this whole thing too seriously, Gareth. Just because I was—taken unawares by what you told me, it doesn't mean that I no longer find Nicolas an attractive man. After all, he is, isn't he? Very attractive, I mean.'

She saw his fingers tighten on the wheel and a wave of exultation swept over her. At last she had succeeded in getting under his skin. It was a small victory, but perhaps it would show him that he was not going to find it so easy to control situations when she had nothing to lose. But that very realisation was almost sufficient to dislodge the small veneer of confidence she had acquired. Still, she had to go on.

'I should imagine any virile married man would find such an isolated life hard to bear,' she remarked idly, casting a casual glance round at the children, who were happily absorbed with some counting game David had invented. 'But a wife doesn't always want to share such a primitive existence, does she? And from what I can see, those men that do bring their wives here come off worst. Was that what went wrong with your marriage, Gareth?'

His fingers were suddenly biting into her knee and his voice was taut as he said: 'That will do, Caroline!'

She looked down at his hand on her leg and a quiver of emotion ran through her. It was true, she thought in amazement, accepting a fact which had hitherto meant little to her. Hate was akin to love, and although he was bruising

84

her it was infinitely better than when he was mocking her. In fact, there was a certain masochistic pleasure about inviting violence that went well with her mood of determined provocation.

'What's the matter?' she queried. 'Was that a little too close to home?'

'Caroline, I warn you ...'

'Oh, yes?' She slanted an amber gaze in his direction. 'And what are you warning me about? Whatever I choose to do or say, you have no authority over me, have you?'

'*Caroline*!' He spoke between clenched teeth, and she allowed a small smile to touch her attractive mouth.

'Don't get so angry, Gareth,' she taunted. 'And please—take your hand off me.'

Gareth removed his hand abruptly to the gear lever, changing down as they descended an incline where a family of baboons blocked the road. For a few minutes he was occupied with dispersing the impudent brood and answering the children's excited questions, but when the vehicle could accelerate again, and David and Miranda were staring wide-eyed out of the rear windows, he said: 'I think I understand what you're trying to do, Caroline, but you won't succeed.'

She frowned. The momentary respite had given him time to compose himself, to rationalise the impulses which she had aroused in him. She glanced impatiently back at the baboons. If only they had not appeared at such an inopportune moment!

She looked down at her hands. There were other ways to disconcert him, of course. There was the oldest way in the world, that of making him aware of her in a wholly physical way, but she doubted her ability to carry it off. And in any case David and Miranda had now lost sight of the baboons and as their counting game had been interrupted they demanded attention.

The remainder of the journey was accomplished without words between Caroline and Gareth, and she was almost glad when they reached the comparative sanctuary of the Laceys' bungalow.

CHAPTER SIX

IT was several days before Caroline saw Gareth again.

Charles had some free time due to him and he decided to take a few days' holiday to show his wife and family a little more of the country around La Vache. Naturally, Caroline accompanied them on these outings, and it was usually left to her to entertain the children while Elizabeth monopolised Charles' attention. Not that Caroline really minded. Apart from the fact that it made things easier all round if Elizabeth was in a good mood, it also enabled Caroline to put thoughts of Gareth to the back of her mind. She refused to consider what her next move would be so far as he was concerned, and waited with an aching kind of impatience for something to happen.

One day they went to visit the mission at Katwe Fork. Laurence Barclay, the missionary, welcomed them warmly, and his wife Helen insisted that they stay for lunch. The Barclays were quite a young couple, in their early forties, Caroline gauged, and she wondered what it was that had made them uproot themselves from a comfortable living in England to this out-of-the-way spot.

After lunch, Helen showed her over the small school. Elizabeth was quite content to relax with the two men while the children had their rest in the Barclays' bedroom, but Caroline, being a teacher herself, was fascinated by the work of these African children. She began to see, as the standard of work increased amongst the older ones, that teaching unformed minds could be quite an incentive.

She complimented Helen on her success, but the older woman deprecated her praise. 'I enjoy it,' she said simply, flicking through the pages of an exercise book. 'These children aren't brainwashed by television, or by the possessions of the child next door. They don't constantly strive to be better than each other, and yet there is a friendly rivalry amongst the older children that makes for good development. Besides, they all want to go to Luanga.'

'The main school,' put in Caroline.

'That's right,' Helen smiled. 'Unfortunately, we can't teach every child who needs to be taught as yet, but I'm hoping that some of my earlier pupils will come back after they've finished their training and help here.'

Caroline examined a charcoal drawing. 'Do you think that's likely?'

Helen shrugged. 'If they're not corrupted by the outside world, I think it's very likely. Unfortunately, every country in Africa is becoming more and more what you would call civilised, and with civilisation comes greed and envy and all the other deadly sins.'

'But surely you're not saying that these people never feel greed or envy?' exclaimed Caroline.

'Oh, no, I'm not saying that. Of course they do. They're human, after all, despite hundreds of years of unformed opinion to the contrary. But the family is important here, every member of it, and therefore there isn't the competition of brother against brother. They don't possess much, but what they do possess is shared—not boasted over. If only people would realise that possessions don't mean a thing. It's people that matter; human relationships. There'd never be the trouble there is in the world if people would only accept a small bite of the apple instead of demanding it all.' She coloured suddenly. 'Oh, dear, I'm sorry, Caroline. I'm making a speech, aren't I? Laurie gets so angry with me for doing this. I shouldn't try to push my ideas on to others. I suppose in its way, it's every bit as bad as the things I'm railing against.'

Caroline smiled. 'Don't be silly, Helen,' she murmured, turning away to look at some pictures pinned to the classroom wall. She didn't want Helen to see her face just then. What she had said made sense. It also illuminated very clearly the things she had said to Gareth seven years ago. 'I—er—I was interested. And I do understand what you're trying to say. Unfortunately, we're imperfect beings in an imperfect world, and there's little we can do about it.'

Helen sighed. 'I know, I know. We can never go back to a state of innocence. I sometimes think even our children are born out of a sense of competitiveness. Certainly we introduce them to such things very early in life—a desire for our child to walk before someone else's, to get its teeth, to eat by itself, to use a potty ... Oh, Caroline, these people see life for what it is—a small space of time before a greater space to come.'

Caroline turned. 'You make it sound very convincing, Helen. Do you have children of your own?'

Helen straightened a pile of textbooks. 'Yes. I have a son, Caroline. He must be twenty-four now.'

Caroline frowned. 'And does he live in Tsaba?'

Helen shook her head. 'No. He lives in England. As far as I know in a small village in Wiltshire.'

'I see.' Caroline sensed she had intruded into some private tragedy and quickly changed the subject. 'How many children are there in the school altogether?'

Helen walked to the blackboard and began to erase the chalked instructions written on it. 'Why don't you ask me why I don't know for certain where my son lives, Caroline?'

Caroline moved awkwardly. 'It's nothing to do with me.'

'Maybe not. But you have every right to ask, all the same. After all, I've just been sounding off to you about families and relationships.'

'Oh, really, Helen——'

The older woman turned. 'No, really, I'd like to tell you. I find you have a sympathetic character, Caroline. You never know—my experience might help you at some future date.'

'It's your personal affair, Helen.'

'I'm not disputing that. But it's no secret, if that's what you're thinking. Michael is our only child. When he was born I was so ill the doctors forbade me ever to have any more children.'

'And did you want more?'

'I wish I had now,' Helen nodded. 'Maybe if we hadn't doted on Michael the way we did—tried to ensure he had the best of everything—clothes, schools, education—he might have turned out differently. But you know how it is. We wanted to equip him as best we could for this competitive world I've been talking about.' She sighed heavily. 'Unfortunately we didn't give Michael much choice in the matter.'

'Helen, please——'

'No, I want to go on.' She shrugged. 'The upshot of it all was that Michael rebelled—in the only way he knew how. By letting us down ... by being expelled from school.' She put down the eraser and rubbed the chalk from her hands. 'You can't imagine how shocked Laurie was—how upset! At first he wouldn't even talk to Michael, and then after I'd begged and cajoled him he did try to come round. I said to give Michael time—that sooner or later he'd find something he wanted to do. I never guessed that something would turn out to be working in a garage in the village in which Laurie had his living.'

'But garage work isn't so bad,' put in Caroline quietly.

'Yes, I know. But Michael was the vicar's son. Greater things were expected of him. Oh, maybe it sounds foolish to you. I suppose it was, but Laurie was always so conscious of what other people thought—of appearances, if you like. He's a good man—but I'm afraid he felt ashamed that his son should let him down so badly.' She looked up. 'Anyway, that wasn't the end of it, as you may have guessed. The garage proprietor's daughter became pregnant—Michael admitted responsibility, and instead of going on to university, making a career for himself, he got married to this—this Eileen Morrison.'

'I see.' Caroline nodded. 'That must have been very distressing for your husband.'

'It was. Oh, Eileen's a pretty girl, but she hasn't a brain in her head. And despite what Michael said at the time, I'm convinced that the marriage won't last. Michael has brains, you see. He simply wouldn't use them to his best advantage. As I say, no doubt we were to blame.'

'I don't think you should blame yourselves entirely,' asserted Caroline firmly. 'After all, there are lots of children who would give their right arm to have his opportunities. I think probably he will live to regret it, but don't you take responsibility for his mistakes.'

Helen half smiled a trifle wistfully. 'Well, anyway, it's all water under the bridge. But that was how we came to leave England. Laurie's work began to suffer dreadfully after Michael got married and then he conceived this idea of coming to Africa.'

'Didn't you mind?' Caroline stared at her admiringly. 'I mean, leaving all your friends—your family?'

'I did at first, yes. I went through a period of blaming first Laurie, then Michael, and finally myself. But now I see my children here developing—I take a share in their somewhat deprived lives—and I'm almost content.'

Caroline looked round the cheerfully decorated room. 'Well, I think you're doing a marvellous job. I just wish—I mean, I envy your courage. Not many women would pack up and start life afresh at—at——'

She halted uncomfortably and Helen laughed, relieving the tension. 'Go on,' she urged. 'Say it! At my age. That's what you meant, didn't you?'

Caroline flushed. 'Well, I meant—after having a child and so on. Not—not everyone would do it.'

'Thankfully not everyone has to,' returned Helen drily, and they walked companionably back to the house.

The children were awake now and in the garden at the back of the mission playing with two black children who Helen explained belonged to her housemaid, Lucy. They were of a similar age to the Laceys' children and while Helen went to make some tea Caroline went to join them.

David and Miranda were trying to teach the others the rudiments of rounders, and called to Caroline to field for them. Goodnaturedly, she agreed, taking up a position at the edge of the cropped area which served as the Barclays' garden. But her attention was soon distracted by a movement in the undergrowth at her feet. Although her skin prickled with apprehension, she had to find out what it was, and bending, she parted the blades of grass to reveal, astonishingly enough, a puppy.

She lifted her head to call David and Miranda to come and see, but the boys had started kicking the ball about and all four children were chasing it across the compound to the schoolhouse. Sighing, she looked again at the puppy, her heart going out to the helpless little animal possibly abandoned here by its mother.

Perhaps they could look after it, she thought. They were to be here several weeks yet. By then it might have grown bigger and strong enough to care for itself. At least the children would love having a pet to care for, and she was fond of animals herself.

With this thought in mind, she went down on her haunches beside the puppy, smiling at it encouragingly, delighting in the limpid depths of its brown eyes. The poor thing was half starved, she saw, its little bones protruding from its skin in places.

She spread the grass again and put her hands under the small body to lift it into her arms. But suddenly sharp little teeth dug painfully into her wrist, and the puppy ran off through the undergrowth.

Caroline gasped and drew back, cradling her injured wrist in her other hand. She looked down. The puppy's teeth had broken the flesh and blood was oozing messily on to her hand.

She got to her feet at once, pulling out a handkerchief and wiping away the blood, cursing herself for being so silly. She ought to have guessed that the creature was no tame domestic animal, that it would defend itself automatically.

She walked back to the mission house and surreptitiously washed her hands at the kitchen sink. Helen was too busy setting out cups and saucers on a tray to pay much attention to her, and Caroline was glad. The last thing she wanted was for anyone to notice what had happened and make a fuss about it. She had been foolish, and when she got back to the bungalow she would cover the punctures with iodine. Fortunately they had all had anti-tetanus injections before leaving England, and she saw no reason to suppose that it would not heal normally.

But by the time she went to bed that night, the bite on her wrist was red and inflamed. She had managed to conceal this fact from Charles and Elizabeth by wearing a long-sleeved blouse at dinner, and afterwards they had gone to the Macdonalds' for an hour or so for drinks. During these days that Charles had been on holiday he had endeavoured to introduce his wife to most of the European population of La Vache, and the fuller social life she was enjoying had reduced Elizabeth's complaints to a minimum.

Caroline made sure she was in bed before the Laceys returned, but she was not asleep. Her wrist throbbed painfully, and even the palliative she had taken had done little to relieve it. Her head ached, and she felt sick, and she wondered miserably whether the animal's teeth had been poisonous.

She heard Charles and Elizabeth go to their room and then the bungalow was silent. Outside, the calls of the night creatures seemed harsher, certainly louder, and the scufflings outside her window seemed more menacing to her increased vulnerability.

She chided herself for allowing her imagination to run away with her. Nothing was any different. It was simply that she was feeling sorry for herself. Yet lying there in the darkness of a moonless night she had the distinct feeling that she hadn't a friend in the world. Who could she turn to in time of trouble? she asked herself tearfully. She had no parents, no blood relations of any kind. There was only Jeremy to care a scrap about her, and she had virtually told him that she wanted nothing more to do with him. The man she had foolishly dreamed might think something of her had made it plain that he disliked and despised her.

She must eventually have slept because she was brought suddenly to consciousness by the clamouring of the children as they scrambled all over her bed. It was broad daylight beyond the shutters on her windows, and the heat was already making the room intolerably hot.

'Come on, Caroline!' Miranda was urging, 'aren't you ever going to get up?'

'It's late,' announced David, tugging the sheet off her. 'Come on! We're hungry!'

Caroline blinked rapidly. The idea of geting up was not appealing. Her head ached abominably, and her tongue felt dry and swollen.

'Oh, give me a chance!' she exclaimed weakly. 'What time is it?'

'It's nearly nine o'clock!' stated David defensively. 'You're always up at eight.'

'I know, I know.' Caroline felt the pain in her wrist but was unable to look at it without attracting the children's attention. 'Go on. Get out of here, and I'll get dressed.'

David regarded her frowningly. 'What's the matter? Are you feeling sick or something?'

'Now why would I be feeling sick?' returned Caroline, forcing a smile. 'Go on. I promise I'm getting up now.'

They went unwillingly, squabbling over who was going to eat the most rolls at breakfast, and Caroline got unsteadily out of bed. Her head swam when first she got to her feet, but gradually the dizziness subsided to be replaced by a dull throbbing somewhere near the base of her scalp. She washed lethargically and as she put on her clothes she recalled that Charles would be back at work today. No doubt Elizabeth wouldn't be seen much before lunch, so she would have to pull herself together and take charge.

Thomas's cheerful face helped a little, but he looked a little surprised to see her wearing the long-sleeved blouse she had worn for dinner the previous evening. Usually she wore the minimum of clothing, and her skin was already honey-tanned.

Refusing any food, she managed to swallow some coffee while the children ate and pretend that nothing was wrong. They chattered away happily and it was not until Miranda dropped the banana she had been peeling and Caroline automatically reached for it that David's sharp eyes noticed the swelling on her wrist.

'Gosh!' he exclaimed, with wide eyes. 'Why is your arm all red and puffy like that?'

Caroline sighed, thrusting her hand down into her lap, hiding the tell-tale injury. 'It's nothing,' she denied, indicating that Miranda should take a fresh banana. 'What are you going to do this morning——'

'I thought you looked sick before,' declared David, not to be diverted. 'Have you had an accident?'

Caroline tried to control her patience, but it was very difficult not to get annoyed when she had tried so desperately to keep the problem to herself and now David was insisting on discussing it.

'It's nothing, David,' she repeated, determinedly taking a sip of her coffee. 'And I wish you'd say no more about it.'

'Why?' David was not to be put off. 'Doesn't Mummy know?'

'No, she doesn't,' said Caroline severely, 'and nor do I want her to. I've told you. Forget about it.'

Miranda put the second half-eaten banana aside. 'Well, I think you should tell Mummy,' she said, in her childish treble. 'It looks awful! I don't like it. It makes me feel sick.'

'Oh, really, Miranda——' Caroline was beginning, trying not to give in to an intense desire to scream at both of them, when there was the sound of a car drawing up outside. David immediately ran to the windows, bouncing up and down excitedly as he shouted:

'Hey, it's Gareth, Miranda. Do you think he's come to take us to the river again?'

Caroline sagged. The very last person she needed to see at this moment was Gareth Morgan. She wasn't strong enough. She couldn't face another confrontation with him, not right now.

She got to her feet shakily, and walked to the door. 'I—I'm going to make the beds,' she said, and both children turned to stare at her in surprise.

'But Gareth's here!'

'He'll want to see you.'

'I doubt it,' replied Caroline, shaking her head.

She had reached her room when she heard the children opening the mesh door, greeting Gareth, asking him why he had come. She closed her door firmly behind her and sought the bed, sinking down on to it weakly. Why had Gareth come? Was he alone? Had he decided to take the children out again now that their father was back at work?

She rested her elbow on the iron end of the bed, supporting her aching head with her hand. She felt pretty rotten and she wondered whether she ought to tell Elizabeth after all. There was Sandra's father, of course. Nicolas had said that Lucas Macdonald was the physician in charge of the men's welfare at the mine. He would know what she should do. Perhaps, after Gareth had gone, she could make an effort and walk to the Macdonalds' house.

Suddenly there was a sharp rap at her door. Instantly she stiffened, but before she had a chance to ask who it was the door opened and Gareth stood there. She supposed he was used to entering a woman's bedroom. He had been married for five or six years when all was said and done, so the appearance of a woman's undergarments could be no surprise to him. Nevertheless, Caroline was not at all used to any man entering her bedroom, least of all one who was regarding her with such anger and frustration.

'Do you mind getting out of here?' she asked coldly, turning so that her back was towards him.

Gareth came into the room instead, walking round her to look down at her with grim eyes. 'What's this I hear about some swelling on your arm?' he demanded. 'Where is it? Let me see!'

Caroline heaved a sigh, showing by the way she was

holding her left arm so stiffly which arm was injured. 'I told the children not to tell anyone——'

'Don't be so damn childish,' he snapped. 'Show me!'

When she didn't make any move to obey him, he came down on the bed beside her, grasping her forearm so that she winced in agony. Then with curiously gentle fingers he unfastened the cuff of her blouse and peeled it back, his lips tightening when he saw the inflamed teethmarks.

'Lord!' he muttered, almost to himself. 'What did this?'

Caroline was feeling slightly faint herself at the sight of the bloated flesh. 'A—a dog,' she breathed unevenly.

'A dog?' he exclaimed impatiently. 'What dog?'

'It—it was a puppy, actually. Yesterday, at—at—the mission.'

'One of those mangy scruffs that Helen insists on feeding, no doubt!' said Gareth shortly. 'I've told her not to encourage the blasted things! It's a wonder she hasn't been bitten herself before now.'

'It—it was no one's fault but my own. I—I tried to pick it up——'

'What!' Gareth stared at her in horror. 'What the hell did you try to do that for?' He shook his head. 'Oh, never mind, I can guess.' He looked down at her wrist again. 'Well, something's got to be done about this—and fast. Tell me, does this hurt—or this?'

He massaged her forearm, but she shook her head, tears trembling on the brink of her eyes.

'Good.' He got to his feet. 'Hang on a minute. I've got a call to make.'

Caroline waited dully for him to come back. She was scarcely aware of David and Miranda coming to stare at her from the opened bedroom door, or of Thomas, sent by Gareth, to shift them away. She remained in a kind of numbed lethargy until Gareth came back again.

He came into the room slowly, clearly intent on his thoughts, and stood looking down at her pensively. Then he said: 'I've spoken to the mine superintendent, but I'm afraid Lucas is away at Luanga today.'

'Lucas?' Caroline was vague. Then she remembered. Of course, Lucas Macdonald!

'It's essential that that swelling is relieved as soon as possible,' he went on. 'Do you want me to do it?'

Caroline's lips parted. 'How?'

'Well, I've no anaesthetic—it's going to be pretty painful—but I wish you'd let me.'

Caroline made a helpless movement of her head. 'Why? Why should you want to help me?' she asked, her voice a trifle shrill. 'I—I thought you hated me!'

Gareth's expression hardened. 'Don't be silly, Caroline. I'd do as much for any human being.'

'Would you? Would you really? Aren't you afraid I'll develop some kind of hero-worship for you? That I might take the fact of your saving my life as some kind of sign on your part——'

'You're being hysterical, Caroline. Look, I realise the fever you're developing is partially responsible, but let's be sensible about this, shall we?'

'Oh, yes, sensible!' Caroline's lips twisted. 'Let's be sensible, by all means!'

'Caroline——' He clenched his fists. 'Are you going to let me——'

'Is she going to let you what? What is going on here? Does no one care that I have the most blinding headache?'

Elizabeth stood swaying in the doorway, Charles's dressing gown wrapped closely about her. She looked at Gareth with an obvious lack of comprehension, and there was a petulant droop to her lips.

Gareth turned. 'Caroline has a swelling on her wrist,' he

explained, with controlled brevity. 'It needs lancing.'

Elizabeth raised a hand to her forehead. 'A swelling,' she repeated helplessly. 'What kind of a swelling?'

'This!' snapped Gareth, losing patience, grasping Caroline's wrist with a distinct lack of gentleness now and displaying it for Elizabeth to see.

'Oh—oh, how revolting!' Elizabeth caught the doorpost dramatically. 'Caroline, in God's name, how did that happen?'

Caroline was weary. There were beads of sweat standing on her smooth brow and her hair had become quite damp. 'A dog bit me,' she replied dully. 'Now will you all go away and leave me alone!'

'No. I don't intend leaving here until something is done about it,' retorted Gareth coldly. 'Caroline, have some sense! Do you want to develop paralysis—or worse?'

Caroline shook her head, tears rolling unchecked down her cheeks. 'Oh, all right,' she agreed weakly, 'all right, do what you have to. I don't care any more.'

Gareth smote his fist against his thigh. 'Right.' He looked at Elizabeth. 'Are you going to help me?'

'Me?' Elizabeth shrank back. 'Heavens, no! I'd be no use. I—I'd faint at the first incision.'

Gareth brushed past her. 'Then get out of the way,' he commanded.

'Well, really——' Elizabeth stared after him indignantly. 'This is our bungalow, after all.'

'Oh, Elizabeth . . .' Caroline shook her head. 'I'm sorry.'

Elizabeth looked at her a moment longer and then with an exasperated gesture she turned and went back to her room.

When Gareth eventually returned, Thomas was with him, his black face unusually grave for once. Gareth handed Caroline a glass containing some amber-coloured liquid and she looked at it in surprise. 'What—what is it?' She sniffed the contents. 'Ugh—it's whisky!'

'Drink it,' advised Gareth quietly. 'This is going to hurt.'

'I don't need whisky,' she declared, putting it down on the bedside table.

Gareth looked as though he was about to argue, but then decided against it. 'Right, then I suggest you look the other way, hmm?'

Caroline turned her head aside. Thomas was given the task of holding her wrist firmly, and she closed her eyes, willing herself not to scream.

It was all over amazingly quickly. The pain was agonising for a few minutes, and she thought she was going to faint, but then the relief that followed was so great that she was able to control her weakness. Gareth wiped away all the pus, sponged it clean with boiled water, and finally applied the salve on a lint dressing. It stung madly, but his hands were firm and cool against her flesh, and so reassuringly competent that she could look at what he was doing without fear.

Although her wrist was still painful, the sick throbbing had gone, and only a powerful weakness in her system remained. The fever had sapped her strength and an intense weariness was stealing over her body. Gareth secured the bandage and then indicated that Thomas should clear everything away. The black servant nodded obligingly, his smile back in evidence, indicating how delighted he was that Caroline was going to be all right.

After he left them, Gareth rose abruptly to his feet, and said: 'I suggest you spend the rest of the day in bed. You look as though you could use some sleep. I don't suppose you slept much last night.'

Caroline shook her head. 'No, I didn't. I—I—I'm very grateful for—for what you've done.'

Gareth raked a hand through his hair which Caroline saw in surprise was soaked with sweat, its lightness artificially darkened. His shirt was sweat-stained, too, dampened around his arms and across his chest where it had touched his skin. She got rather unsteadily to her feet, and put out a hand, touching his upper arm, feeling the muscles tauten beneath the fine cotton.

'Gareth——' she began huskily, but he stepped back, away from her.

'Don't touch me, Caroline,' he said harshly, and her eyes clouded with pain.

'I'm sorry,' she whispered, scarcely understanding why. 'I—I just wanted to thank you.'

He glanced towards the open doorway. 'There's no need.'

'Oh, but there is,' she insisted. 'I—I was foolish. I—I suppose it was because—well, I didn't want to—owe you anything.'

'You don't.'

She took a step toward him. 'But I do.' She allowed her fingers to trail down his shirt front, tempted to unfasten the buttons and touch his heated flesh. 'It's obvious from this——' She indicated the sweat stains. 'It's obvious that you've been under quite a strain.' She paused, looking up at him, noticing the way a nerve was jerking at his jawline. 'Was it very abhorrent—touching me?'

'I think this has gone far enough, Caroline,' he muttered, his hands clenched by his sides. 'You'd better get to bed, and I'll make sure that Lucas comes to see you the minute he gets back from Luanga.'

Caroline's eyes moved over him slowly. 'And how will you do that?' she asked provocatively. 'By speaking to Sandra?' She tilted her head to one side. 'Is it true? Are you—attracted to her?'

She didn't know what had made her say that. Perhaps the

strain she had been under and the sudden relief which had followed had loosened her tongue, but she saw a darkening of angry colour in his cheeks at her words.

'Don't try me too far, Caroline,' he said savagely. 'There are limits to my endurance and right now I've almost reached them. I'm glad my efforts on your behalf have proved so beneficial. Unfortunately, that's as far as my concern stretches. Nor do I intend to satisfy your warped curiosity about my relationship with Sandra, except to tell you that she's an infinitely warmer person than you'll ever be!'

'You speak from experience, I suppose,' she remarked sarcastically, hating him for being able to hurt her so easily still.

Gareth shrugged. 'If you choose to think so.'

'Of course. She's a homely girl, isn't she? Exactly your type!' She was not usually a spiteful person, but his words had caught her on the raw.

He gave her a contemptuous look. 'Oh, yes, I'll grant you Sandra's no fashion-plate. But then she's no ogre either. She doesn't have your looks—your flair for clothes. But she has warmth and sincerity, and she doesn't judge her friends by the size of their bank balance.'

'That's a filthy thing to say!' declared Caroline indignantly, and swung her uninjured hand towards his face in a gesture of impulsive anger.

But he caught her wrist easily enough, preventing her from striking him, holding her off, his grip hard and unyielding. 'I think not,' he remarked coldly, and her lips trembled. 'Such outraged dignity is a little out of place in someone without morals or scruples!'

'You know nothing about my morals, and you're not so scrupulous yourself!'

'What do you mean?' His hold tightened painfully.

'I don't believe you're as indifferent to me as you like to

103

pretend,' she cried. 'The things I've said and done wouldn't mean a thing to you if you really were as insensitive as you'd like to believe.' Her amber eyes narrowed, the long dark lashes casting shadows on the pale, creamy skin of her cheeks. 'I wonder what you'd do, Gareth, if I chose to make —demands on you.'

Gareth pushed her away from him then, so violently that she had to grasp the iron bedpost for support. 'I shouldn't advise you to try anything, Caroline,' he bit out furiously, and before she could make any reply he strode out of the room.

CHAPTER SEVEN

LUCAS MACDONALD put Caroline on a course of injections which necessitated her attending his house every evening for treatment. It was terribly embarrassing for her. She felt that she was being a nuisance, a feeling which was not relieved by Sandra Macdonald's attitude. She had made it plain that she considered Caroline's behaviour as little short of criminally careless, and both she and her father had applauded Gareth's handling of a potentially dangerous situation. Even Elizabeth, when she recovered from being ordered about in her own home, had to admit that she didn't know what they would have done without his assistance.

At least the incident had served to put Caroline on her guard, not only with herself but with the children, and she warned them against touching anything, no matter how appealing it might seem.

Although she had thought that perhaps Gareth might come back to see how his patient was faring she was disappointed, but two days afterwards Nicolas Freeleng turned up. He came in the afternoon while the children were resting and found Caroline and Elizabeth stretched out in the shade at the back of the house reading magazines.

'Good afternoon, ladies!' he greeted them gallantly, standing surveying them with obvious pleasure. 'And how is the invalid today?'

Caroline levered herself into an upright position. 'If you're meaning me, I'm not an invalid,' she answered coolly.

'Oh, but I understand there was quite a panic on a

couple of days ago,' he parried. 'I've been away for a few days, but when I got back and heard what had happened, I had to come and see for myself.'

Elizabeth shrugged her shoulders impatiently. 'Caroline was bitten by some mangy animal at the Barclays', that was all. Gareth managed to lance the infected area and prevent blood poisoning.'

'Ah, yes, Gareth,' Nicolas nodded, looking down at Caroline. 'How fortunate that he happened along at just the right moment!'

Elizabeth sniffed. 'We never did find out why he came, did we, Caroline?'

Caroline shook her head, frowning, but Nicolas nudged her foot with his. 'And are you fully recovered now, pussycat?'

Elizabeth's brows ascended at this casual form of address, and Caroline couldn't help looking embarrassed. 'Yes, I'm fine, thank you,' she replied.

'But I understand you're having injections.'

'You seem to know everything,' she remarked, rather dryly.

Nicolas smiled, 'That's my job, pussycat.' He went down on his haunches beside the cane chair on which she was lying. 'I wondered whether you might care to have dinner with me this evening.'

Caroline looked at Elizabeth, who was looking even more put out. 'I'm afraid not,' she refused quietly.

The corners of Nicolas's mouth turned down. 'Why not?'

Caroline looked at him squarely. 'I think you know why not.'

Nicolas held her gaze. 'I want to talk to you—to explain——'

Caroline shook her head and looked away from him. 'Not tonight,' she insisted firmly.

106

Nicolas drew in a deep breath and rose to his feet, his eyes on Elizabeth, inducing her to leave them. She fought the penetration of his silent demands for several minutes, but then she got rather jerkily to her feet.

'I'll see about some tea,' she announced shortly, and walked into the bungalow.

After she had disappeared inside, Nicolas drew the chair she had been using nearer to Caroline and sat in it himself. 'Now,' he said, 'we can talk.'

'I don't see what we have to talk about.'

'Don't you?'

'No.' She ran her fingers over her knees. 'You're married, Nicolas, and that's that.'

'Why are you being so unkind to me? Marriage doesn't necessarily mean happiness, you know.'

'Oh, please—don't give me that my-wife-doesn't-understand-me routine! I don't particularly care what kind of a relationship you have with your wife. The fact that she exists is enough.'

Nicolas tried to take her hand, but she evaded him and he scowled. 'What's the matter? You're so cold—so aloof! Can you not accept that a man like myself needs female companionship? Just because I'm married it doesn't mean that I don't find you disturbingly attractive!'

Caroline felt angry with him. 'Well, I'm afraid I don't get involved with married men.'

Nicolas shrugged. 'I assure you, my wife wouldn't mind.'

'But I would!' Caroline was astounded. 'I don't know how you have the nerve to come here and tell me such a thing! If this is what you meant by explaining—well, I'm sorry, but I don't accept your explanations.'

He pressed his balled fist into his palm. 'But why? Caroline, you're only here for a few weeks. Why shouldn't we have a little fun together? Surely a young woman like yourself wouldn't wish to spend these weeks solely in the company of children!'

'There are other people here,' she pointed out shortly.

'Who? The Laceys? The Hollands? The Macdonalds? I don't somehow see you having a great deal of fun with any of them. There's Jonas, of course, but he's a little young for you, I think.'

'I have no desire to discuss my social life with you,' she declared. 'How I spend my time is my concern and mine only.'

Nicolas exhaled noisily. 'Don't you think your attitude is a little old-fashioned? Why, even Sandra Macdonald sees no harm in her association with Gareth.'

Caroline's nerve-ends tingled. 'But Gareth's not married,' she ejaculated.

Nicolas made a moue. 'Not now, perhaps. But he was.'

Caroline felt something screwing her up inside. 'Well ——' she began, 'well, Sandra Macdonald's affairs are no concern of mine.'

'Won't you at least have dinner with me?' he pleaded.

'No.'

'Not even if I promise that there'll be at least half a dozen other people present?'

Caroline opened her mouth to refuse and then closed it again. 'I—I don't know,' she said, suddenly alert.

Nicolas was encouraged by her indecision. 'Please. Say you will. I'll even invite the Laceys so that you'll be sure of getting home safely.'

She had to smile at this, a tremulous, uneasy kind of smile that denoted her extreme state of tension had he been aware of it. 'When—when are you having this dinner party?'

'Well, as I'm to have so many guests, I'd better make it tomorrow,' he conceded reluctantly. 'But you will come, won't you? Promise?'

'All right,' she nodded. But all she was thinking was that tomorrow she would see Gareth again. He was bound to be one of the guests, and her spirits lifted even while she despised them for doing so.

But Gareth did not attend the dinner party.

It was arranged that David and Miranda should sleep at the Macdonalds' as a special treat and so save Sandra the necessity of spending the evening alone at the Laceys' bungalow, and when Caroline took the children along with her when she went for her evening injection she found Gareth lounging lazily on a couch in their living-room. To say she was shocked would have been an understatement, but her reaction was partially concealed by the children's delight at seeing him again.

'Are you sleeping here, too?' asked David eagerly, and Caroline bent her head to hide the hot colour that suddenly burned in her cheeks. Why, oh, why had she agreed to go to Nicolas's dinner party? She didn't want to go. She had no interest in socialising for its own sake. She had expected to see Gareth. And now he was here ...

Gareth had got to his feet at their entrance and Lucas, who had admitted them, said: 'Come along, Caroline. Let's get the unpleasant part of the evening over straight away.'

Caroline nodded, and without looking again at Gareth she accompanied the doctor through to the small room at the back which he used as a kind of surgery. It was the room in the Laceys' bungalow which Caroline occupied, but of course the Macdonalds only needed two bedrooms.

She scarcely felt the injection. She felt numb, and Lucas looked at her a trifle anxiously. 'Are you feeling all right?' he asked. 'You've not had any after-effects of the treatment, have you? No pain or paralysis?'

109

'Oh, no—no!' Caroline shook her head, forcing a smile. 'I feel fine, honestly.'

Lucas was thoughtful. 'You know, I think the heat's getting to you at last,' he said. 'You do too much, you know. Those children should be with their parents more. I've even heard that you do their washing.'

'How do you know that?' Caroline was astonished.

Lucas smiled, and opening the door he switched off the surgery light. 'We have a very reliable grapevine,' he chuckled. 'Actually, Caroline, it was your houseboy Thomas who told ours. They're cousins, you see.'

'Oh,' Caroline nodded, and they walked back along the hall towards the lounge. 'Well, I must be going. There's no need to walk me home tonight, Mr. Macdonald. See you tomorrow.'

'Don't be silly. I wouldn't dream of allowing you to walk home alone,' exclaimed Lucas. 'Besides, Gareth's here. Come and have a drink with us first.'

'Oh, really, I——' she began, but Lucas had re-entered the lounge where Gareth was on his knees helping David to load matchsticks into a toy cannon he had brought with him. As they entered, Gareth stood up and said:

'I'll walk Caroline home, Lucas. I'd enjoy the exercise.'

'Well, stay and have a drink first,' exclaimed Lucas. 'Where's Sandra?'

'She's preparing supper,' replied Gareth, fastening the top buttons of his navy cotton shirt. 'Do you want her?'

'No, perhaps I'd better not disturb her,' murmured Lucas, doubtfully.

'Look, I'll go,' said Caroline. 'I'll see you tomorrow.' She flicked a glance in Gareth's direction. 'There's no need for you to come. It's only a few yards.'

Gareth ignored her, however, and went ahead as she was saying goodbye to the children to open the mesh door for her to precede him outside. Once in the open air, however, Caroline put on speed, and almost ran down the path to the road. Gareth quickened his pace to catch up with her, but then his hand closed round her forearm, slowing her progress considerably. It was the injured arm he held, and she gasped as the sudden tightening of his fingers sent a sliver of pain through her hand.

'I'm sorry,' he muttered impatiently, sensing her withdrawal, but he did not release her. 'I don't want to hurt you, but I do want to talk to you, and if you continue to race like this I shan't have the chance.'

Caroline was forced to slow down. 'I'd rather hurry. I have to get ready to go out.'

'Yes. That's what I want to talk to you about.' Gareth halted abruptly. 'You're going to Nick's tonight, aren't you?'

'What if I am?' She sounded cool, but inside she was a seething mass of burning sensations.

'I thought you would have had more sense!' he snapped.

'What do you mean?' She assumed a defiant stance. 'Everyone needs attention sometimes, and it's really rather flattering to know that a man like Nicolas finds me so attractive! Why, even you need a woman's companionship, don't you, Gareth? What kind of cosy evening do you intend to have, I wonder? And you forgot to answer David's question, didn't you? Are you going to sleep there?'

'Why, you insolent little——' He bit off an epithet. 'I'd like to——'

'What would you like to do, Gareth?' she taunted him, as he paused. 'Do tell me. I'm dying to know!'

His tension was evident in the hardening pain of his grip on her arm, like a physical presence about them. 'I'd like to put you over my knee!' he spoke savagely. 'Maybe that kind of punishment would teach you some respect.

111

It's certain that your mother didn't teach you any, more's the pity.'

'Leave my mother out of this!'

'Why should I?' Gareth was scornful. 'She has a hell of a lot to answer for.'

Caroline was a little scared of the violence she had aroused in him now. 'Will you please let go of me, Gareth? Your—your girl-friend will be wondering what's taking you so long——'

Gareth looked down at her, the anger in his expression discernible even in the gloom. Diffused light from a bungalow window some few feet away illuminated the spot where they were standing, and with a muffled exclamation he dragged her out of that revealing radiance and into the shadow of a clump of bushes which edged someone's garden. Then he released her arm to take her by the shoulders and shake her quite violently.

'What is it you want, Caroline?' he demanded, in a tortured voice. 'What will satisfy you? If you're so desperate for masculine admiration perhaps I should oblige you. I'm afraid I'm not conversant with all the modern trends. I foolishly imagined that you desired a more permanent relationship. It seems I was wrong, and as you're an attractive woman, I see no reason to deny myself what's so freely offered——'

Caroline gasped, his words acting on her like a douche of cold water. 'How—how dare you——?' she began, but he was not listening to her. His hands had slid round her neck, his thumbs against the pulses which beat so erratically beneath that increasing pressure. For a moment when he looked into her eyes she sensed a kind of self-contempt behind his anger, but then his mouth touched hers and her lips parted convulsively.

She tried to resist him. This was not the way she had

planned that he should want her. This was not what she had flown half across the world for. But it was a disurbingly accurate facsimile, and she realised she had forgotten exactly how expert he was at making love. Maybe if he had been ungentle with her, if he had sought to subdue her by violent means, she would have been able to withstand him, but his mouth explored hers with growing passion, and his hands slid down over her shoulderblades to rest on her hips, holding her firmly against him.

Weakness invaded her system, and she sank against him helplessly, feeling the instant hardening of his body. Her hands were crushed against his chest, but she felt no pain. The muscles of his thighs were against hers, but even the thinness of their garments seemed too great a barrier between them. She pressed herself against him. Why resist when all her senses cried out for a fulfilment only he could assuage? She heard his hoarse protestations as she yielded against him that belied the desperation behind his touch, but then he tore himself away from her, leaving her utterly bereft.

'Oh, *God*!' he cursed savagely, raking his scalp with his nails. 'What kind of a man do you think I am? How much of this do you think I can stand? Would you have me lose control completely— make love to you here—where anyone can see us?'

'Gareth——'

'No! No, for God's sake, don't say anything,' he commanded, lines of strain visible around his mouth. 'Go to your dinner party! It seems I was wrong. Nick is better equipped to deal with you than I am!'

'What do you mean?' She stared at him in dismay.

Gareth shook his head. 'Maybe you're two of a kind,' he spoke almost to himself. 'You each care more for yourselves than you do for anyone else.'

113

'That's not true——'

'Isn't it?' Gareth turned away from her. 'You don't care what you do—who you hurt—so long as *you* get what you want. It's an unfortunate quality you both possess.'

'Gareth, please——' She wrung her hands helplessly. 'I couldn't help myself a few minutes ago, any more than you could. It just happened. It was always like that between us. Don't you remember?'

Gareth thrust his hands deep into the waist pockets of his navy trousers. 'The Laceys' bungalow is just across the road. If you'll walk across, I'll remain here until you're safely inside.'

'Oh, Gareth, you can't pretend it never happened! I didn't plan it, if that's what you're thinking.'

'Indirectly you did.'

'How? In what way?'

'If you hadn't come here, if you hadn't deliberately sought me out, we would never, in all probability, have laid eyes on one another again.'

'You think not?'

He shrugged. 'Well, I concede it's a remote possibility. We might have met accidentally if ever I went to England to see my sister. But it would have been nothing more than a casual encounter.'

'You can't deny that you—that you wanted to kiss me just now,' she cried.

Gareth's lips twisted. 'No. I can't deny that.'

'And—and if things had been different—if we'd been somewhere else, you might—you might have——'

'I might have what, Caroline?' His eyes were hard and cold. 'Made love to you?' He looked unpleasantly at her. 'All right. I won't embarrass you by questioning the validity of that remark.'

'You—you *swine*!' Caroline couldn't believe her ears. She couldn't believe that he could change so completely from the hungry, passionate lover he had been only minutes ago into this cold, calculating brute who was making her feel cheap and dirty. Her arm had begun to throb from the pressure he had exerted on it earlier and the need to make him believe her was being swamped by a strong sense of self-pity. She had urgent desire to burst into tears, but to do so in front of him was to invite further sarcasm. He had already told her what he thought of her tears.

Summoning all her composure she turned away, looking up and down the track. It was only a few yards to the Laceys' bungalow. Surely she could reach it without giving way to emotionalism. She set off jerkily, and then was almost defeated when he called: 'Goodnight.'

Goodnight! The word sang in her ears. That he should treat her as he had done and then expect her to say goodnight as though there had been nothing more than casual conversation between them!

She didn't answer him. She couldn't. She was too choked up. And the idea of Nicolas's dinner party didn't bear thinking about ...

During the following week, both David and Miranda went down with gastric tummies. Elizabeth, who left all the washing of stained sheets to Caroline, blamed Thomas's cooking, but if she hoped to bludgeon Caroline into doing that as well she was sadly disappointed. The younger girl had enough to do running about after two demanding invalids, and so Elizabeth herself tackled a few simple meals for her family.

The days were passing absurdly quickly. It was almost three weeks since they had come to Tsaba, and Caroline would not allow herself to consider that in three weeks she would be home again, in London, never to see Gareth again.

Nicolas was a frequent visitor at the bungalow in spite of the fact that Caroline would have little to do with him. He brought candies and presents for the children, and once a box of Turkish Delight for Elizabeth, but Caroline knew they were only excuses. He really came to see her, and while it was rather flattering, as she had told Gareth, it was also rather annoying. She didn't want to see Nicolas, she didn't want his admiration; and nor did she care to speculate on what Gareth must be thinking if Nicolas told him how often he came to La Vache.

Her arm had healed now, and was no longer painful to the touch, but she still continued with the injections Lucas had prescribed. That was the part of the day she cared for least, when occasionally she saw Sandra Macdonald and had to listen to her talking about Gareth. She was half convinced that the other girl suspected that she felt something for the attractive civil engineer and deliberately chose to discuss Gareth when she was around to show how close they were. And probably Sandra spoke nothing but the truth—Gareth was often at the Macdonalds' house, and it seemed generally expected among the European population that it was only a matter of time before they got married.

From time to time, Caroline found herself speculating upon their relationship before Gareth's wife left him. She couldn't help but wonder what had precipitated their separation, and the idea that Sandra might have had something to do with it made her feel slightly sick. She had never met Gareth's ex-wife, although she had heard about her from her mother. She had lost no time in taunting Caroline about it, claiming that she had been right all along, that Gareth was no different from any other man, that he hadn't really loved her at all or he wouldn't have been willing to put someone else in her place so swiftly. At that time it had seemed an inescapable conclusion, and Caroline had secretly cried herself to sleep for nights on end knowing that her chance to effect a reconciliation with Gareth was irrevocably destroyed.

On Friday, at the end of that hectic week, Charles took the day off. He suggested that as the children were up and about again, albeit looking a little peaky still, they might take a picnic lunch out with them and go and visit Kywari game reserve some forty miles away. Elizabeth was mildly enthusiastic and naturally the children were excited, but Caroline was not so keen. It had been an exhausting week for her and the idea of a day alone did not come amiss.

'You go,' she said. 'I'll stay here.'

'But you'll miss seeing the elephants!' exclaimed David in consternation. 'Daddy says we might see a rhi— rhicerus—' He looked appealingly towards his father. 'What is it?'

'A rhinoceros,' said Charles obligingly. 'Why don't you just say rhino?'

'All right.' David turned back to Caroline. 'We might see a rhino!' His eyes were large. 'And Daddy says there are always lots of zebras and giraffes to be seen. Won't you come?'

Caroline smiled gently at him, touched at his concern. 'I don't think so, thank you, David.'

'Why not?' Miranda chimed in. 'You've always come before.'

'Caroline's had a pretty busy week with you two,' said Charles firmly. 'I don't know what your mother would have done without her. So let her have a nice peaceful day without you two constantly clamouring for attention.'

'Would you mind?' Caroline looked at Elizabeth.

Elizabeth looked at her husband and then, reading his expression, shook her head. 'No, of course not. You've scarcely had any free time since we came here, except in the evenings, of course. We'll cope, I suppose. I just hope Charles knows what he's doing taking our two into a game reserve. You have to remain in the car, you know, David. You can't go bounding madly about like you do at home.'

David nodded. 'I know, I know. Daddy told me already.'

Elizabeth gave her son an exasperated pat on the nose. 'You always know everything, don't you, pest?' she asked goodhumouredly, and David giggled delightedly.

After they had gone the bungalow seemed extraordinarily quiet. Caroline realised that it was the first time she had had the place to herself since their arrival, and for once she had no one to consider but herself. Of course, Thomas was still pottering about, but she had decided to dismiss him at lunchtime and make a meal herself for the others returning home.

The morning stretched ahead of her, delightfully empty of all responsibilities, and she tucked her thumbs into the low belt of her hipster shorts and mooched through to the living room. What to do, that was the immediate problem.

She lounged into a chair, draping one leg inelegantly over an arm, and rested her chin on her hand. Why was it that the idea of being able to spend a day in bed had such appeal when one was being overloaded with responsibilities, and yet became such a waste of a day when the occasion presented itself? She couldn't go to bed now. It was a glorious morning outside. How could she deny its appeal by burying herself between the sheets?

She sighed. If only she had some means of transport, she thought regretfully. She could have gone for a drive. It would have been quite an adventure—on her own.

She rose to her feet again and walked across the room, catching sight of her reflection in the mirror near the door. She did look pale, she conceded reluctantly. There were definite signs of weariness around her eyes, and her hair had a lacklustre quality.

That was because it needed washing, she decided, glad to have a definite objective in mind. She would wash her hair and dry it in the sun. That would be a nice, inexhausting thing to do.

It was fortunate that Caroline's hair required no special effort. At home, if she wanted it to look especially nice, she put rollers in the ends to give it more bounce, but since coming to Africa she had merely washed it and allowed it to dry straight. It still had the tendency to curve under her chin and was so thick and silky that it always looked attractive.

She washed it in the basin in the bathroom with some lukewarm water Thomas provided. Then she rubbed it almost dry and emerged to find a brush and comb. She was standing in the hall, binding the towel more securely round her head, when a man's outline appeared beyond the mesh door at the end, and her heart flipped a beat. It was Gareth, and after giving a peremptory knock, he simply opened the door and walked in.

Caroline was taken aback. She wished desperately that he had not seen her like this, her head swathed in a towel, her eyes reddened from the invasion of the shampoo. But she could not avoid him. Short of diving into her bedroom like a scared rabbit there was nothing to do but stand there and make the best of it.

Gareth drew off the dark glasses he had worn to protect his eyes, and she took a couple of steps forward. 'What do you want?' she demanded, and then coloured under his intent scrutiny. He made her feel embarrassingly aware of the limitations of her appearance, and she laid a protective arm across her breasts, thinly concealed beneath the white bra top of her bikini.

'Where is everyone?' he enquired, her defensive action causing a mocking lift to his lips.

'Charles and Elizabeth have taken the children to the Kywari game reserve.'

'Indeed?' Gareth looked through into the living-room. 'So you're on your own, then.'

'Thomas is in the kitchen!' she declared, and Gareth half smiled.

'Is he really?' he commented. 'And why didn't you go to the game reserve?'

'I—I was tired. The children have been ill. It's been quite a hectic week.'

Gareth inclined his head. 'Yes,' he murmured thoughtfully, 'you do look rather pale. I heard from Nick that you've been working like a slave—er—his words, not mine.'

Caroline coloured. 'Is that all?'

Gareth raised dark eyebrows, and strolled uninvited into the lounge. 'Aren't you being rather ungracious?' he asked, stretching his length comfortably in a low chair.

Caroline had been forced to come down the hall to speak to him and now she stood in the doorway uncomfortably shifting her weight from one foot to the other. 'What are you doing?' she cried. 'I've just washed my hair——'

'I had noticed.'

'—and I have to dry it!'

'Is that all that's pricking you?' enquired Gareth, regarding her uneasy stance with pointed irony, and immediately Caroline was still.

'Look, Gareth,' she said, with burning cheeks, 'I don't know what your game is, but I wish you would leave—now!'

'Don't be so unneighbourly, Caroline. I understand—certain other guests, who shall remain nameless, get very different treatment.'

'If you're meaning Nicolas Freeleng, I don't ask him to come here.'

'But you don't discourage him either.'

'What am I supposed to say to him? He is Charles's employer, you know.'

Gareth swung himself to his feet. 'All right, all right. I don't intend to spend the whole day arguing over Nick Freeleng. That's not why I came.'

'Why did you come?' Caroline spread a hand. 'You didn't seem surprised when I told you that the Laceys weren't here.'

'I wasn't.'

Caroline gasped. 'You mean—you knew they'd gone out for the day?'

'As a matter of fact, yes. I passed them on the road here. Charles shouted across that they were going to Kywari.'

Caroline shook her head. 'Then why did you come here pretending you didn't know?'

Gareth ran a hand round the back of his neck. 'Would you believe—to see you?'

Caroline had to grasp the door jamb for support. 'What?'

Gareth shrugged. 'Well, why not? I got to thinking that in a couple of weeks you'll be going back to England, and I thought how stupid it was to go on with this feud. I mean—I don't care to be hated too much.'

Caroline tugged the towel from her hair with nervous

fingers, allowing the damp tendrils to fall unheeded about her bare neck. 'I see,' she managed at last. 'So you came to apologise.'

Gareth sighed. 'No, not to apologise,' he stated rather impatiently. 'Just to make peace between us.'

CHAPTER EIGHT

THERE was silence for several minutes as Caroline digested this and then she said slowly: 'And am I supposed to respond?'

Gareth's hand fell to his side. 'That's up to you. I've said what I came to say.'

'You've absolved your conscience, is that it? For what happened a week ago?'

Gareth had the grace to colour slightly. 'My conscience is clear,' he said steadily, but she sensed he was holding himself in control.

Turning away, she touched her hair almost absently. Her thoughts were running riot. This was the very last thing she would have expected him to do. To attempt to create a kind of anonymous relationship between them. But he had, and that in itself created a whole new spectrum of possibilities.

'Well,' she murmured, flicking a glance in his direction, 'as you are here, perhaps you would like a drink—beer, I mean, or some coffee.'

Gareth hesitated. 'I thought you wanted to dry your hair.'

'It's almost dry already,' she replied. 'It won't take a minute to make some coffee. Do say you'll have some.'

She had placed him in the defensive position now, and he gave a helpless gesture. 'Very well.'

Thomas soon prepared a tray and Caroline carried it back to the living room. Gareth was standing staring out of the window, but he came to a chair at her invitation, and accepted a cup of coffee without comment.

Caroline sat opposite him on the couch, sipping her coffee, surveying him unobtrusively over the rim of her cup. Then she said: 'Why did you come down to La Vache?'

Gareth replaced his cup on the tray. 'I had some medical supplies which I'd promised to bring down for Lucas.'

'Oh, I see.' Caroline offered him more coffee, but he refused. 'And are you going back to Nyshasa now?'

'That's right.'

'Take me with you!'

'What?' Gareth rose abruptly to his feet.

'Take me with you.' Caroline looked up at him innocently. 'I've never seen the construction site. I'd like to. And I've got nothing to do today.'

Gareth took a deep breath. 'A construction site is no place for a woman. Besides, I should have to bring you back again. I don't have that much time to waste.'

Caroline lifted her eyebrows. 'Then I'd ask Nicholas,' she replied calmly. 'I'm sure he'd bring me home.'

She saw the way Gareth's knuckles had whitened as his fists clenched by his sides. It was obvious that his idea of creating a peaceful relationship between them had not covered every eventuality.

'Caroline, this is ridiculous, and you know it!'

'Why?' She stood up. 'Where's the harm? As you pointed out, I shall be back in England very soon. Surely taking me to see the construction site doesn't present such an insuperable obstacle.'

Gareth shook his head. 'Caroline, I came here with the sole intention of putting things between us on to a normal footing. I said that continuing to behave as we were doing was stupid. But that doesn't mean that I want your company any more now than I did before!'

Caroline refused to let him see that he could hurt her so easily. If this conversation deteriorated into a slanging match as it was likely to do if she attempted to retaliate she might just as well give up all hope of Gareth ever taking her anywhere, of having anything more to do with her. She had to remain sweet and reasonable, and not allow him to twist the situation to suit his own ends.

'But, Gareth,' she protested appealingly, 'I'm not asking much. This is the first opportunity I've had to go anywhere without the children since we came here. It's not as if I'm asking you to—well, take me out for a meal or anything. I'm a teacher. I'd be interested to see the dam.'

Gareth chewed his lower lip. 'Would you?'

'Yes. Besides, if we can maintain a civil conversation I've no doubt you'd be interested to hear how things have changed back home in England. Oh, please, Gareth ... Prove you mean what you say.'

Gareth regarded her with obvious misgivings. 'Very well, Caroline,' he conceded at last, 'I'll take you to the site. But you'll have to put some more clothes on. I have no intention of taking a half-naked white woman with me!'

Caroline hid her elation. 'Just give me five minutes,' she asserted, her voice sounding reassuringly unconcerned. 'Have another cup of coffee.'

In her room, she rummaged through the chest impatiently, coming up with a pair of pink hipster jeans and a sleeveless purple sweater. She threw off her shorts and pulled the jeans and sweater on over her bikini. Then she brushed her hair vigorously, relieved to see that it was already almost dry. She caught it up off her neck with a navy ribbon, and after a swift appraising glance at herself in the spotted mirror she was ready.

Gareth took in the attractive picture she made in silence, and then indicated the door. 'I've told Thomas where you're going,' he remarked as they walked out to the car.

In spite of the fact that Gareth spoke very little Caroline enjoyed the drive to Nyshasa. He was a much more competent driver than either Charles or Nicolas and he handled the powerful station wagon with cool confidence. Once a deer crossed their path, and Caroline exclaimed at its gentle appearance.

'You never know what you're going to encounter on these roads, do you?' she laughed. 'Have you ever met anything awkward—like a leopard, or a lion—or even an elephant? And aren't rhinos supposed to be dangerous!'

'You have a very vivid imagination,' remarked Gareth dryly. 'This isn't a safari park, you know.'

Caroline refused to allow him to dampen her enthusiasm. 'But there are wild animals about, aren't there?'

'Yes,' agreed Gareth mildly. 'But the big cats are too fond of their own skin to risk being run down by a car, and we don't see many elephants about here.'

'Oh!' Caroline hunched her shoulders.

Gareth half smiled. 'You remind me of David,' he said. 'You imagine every outing is a big game hunt!'

'I don't,' protested Caroline, forgetting their differences for once and speaking impulsively. 'I just thought one had to take care, that's all.'

'Oh, one does,' exclaimed Gareth, gently mocking. 'But no rhino's going to come and horn us off the road or anything dramatic like that.'

'How do you know?'

'The rhino is a rather unkindly-regarded animal. It's not half as black as it's painted. It's very short-sighted, and has to go entirely on its sense of smell. I'm not saying that if you interfered with its way of life it wouldn't come charging across at you to defend itself, but that's all. It's not blatantly malicious.'

'Have you ever been charged by a rhino?'

Gareth shook his head. 'I'm afraid not.'

'Have you had any dangerous encounters with animals, then?'

'I had a brush with an elephant once,' commented Gareth reflectively. 'But Africa's no longer one enormous game reserve, Caroline. There are too many get-rich-quick merchants trading in skins and ivory for the really valuable species to survive much longer.'

Caroline nodded. 'It's such a shame. Why do people always want what they can't have?'

Gareth's fingers tightened on the steering wheel. 'A good question,' he murmured, and she sensed his double meaning.

The construction site was some distance above the falls where the Kinzori forked. It was a hive of activity when they arrived. The enormous concrete structure was already reaching some distance across the fork, baulking the flow of water, a network of iron girders and overhead cranes. The air was thick with dust and there was the constant scream of power drills and the whine of mixers. Caroline had no idea how many men were employed at the site, but there seemed hundreds from what she could see. Some were working on the reinforced structure, while others crawled along the rough gantry which pontooned the river at this point. All around was evidence of a razing of the vegetation of the area, a great man-made clearing that defied the encompassing mass of the jungle. There was something unreal about such a development here, miles from any real civilisation, and it was difficult to accept that without the dam, without the hydro-electric plant which would follow, there could be no real progress. All the same, in its way, it was every bit as alien to this part of Africa as the illicit traders, destroying to a certain extent the animals' way of life. If a hydro-electric plant was built here, if civilisation as she knew it flourished, where would the wild animals go? It was an insoluble problem.

Gareth brought the station wagon to a halt and climbed out without a word. Immediately two men converged on him from different directions, each concerned with some problem that required his attention. Gareth listened to what they had to say, standing between them, lean and indolent, his hands resting lightly on his hips. In a cream denim shirt and narrow fitting mud-coloured denim pants he looked disturbingly attractive, and Caroline forced herself to climb out of the car to evade such disruptive thoughts. She stood watching the group who had their backs to her feeling decidedly *de trop* in a man's world, a feeling which was increased when Gareth seemed to forget her presence altogether and began walking with his colleagues towards a wooden building set to one side of the site. Caroline had seen such buildings on sites back home. They were used by engineers and the like for progress drawings and consultations.

She looked about her a trifle unhappily, aware of several pairs of dark eyes watching her with interest. Reaching into the station wagon, she took out a pair of enormous sunglasses, sliding them on to her nose firmly. They provided a small screen between her and her audience, but she wished that Gareth would look round and remember he had brought a visitor.

To her dismay, the men disappeared inside the building and she was left alone to view her surroundings. She wondered whether Gareth expected her to sit in the station wagon and wait until he had time to notice her. It was hot and stuffy in the stationary vehicle and she hadn't come all this way just to sit in a car.

Instead, she wandered a few steps towards the mess of men and machinery that flanked the fast moving waters of the Kinzori, looking up at the vast wall of reinforced concrete which would eventually stem the divided flow of the river. It was fascinating watching the men moving with sure-footed ease along iron girders no wider than a man's hand, high above the ground, and she paid no attention when she heard angry shouting behind her. It was not until a firm hand grasped her arm, swinging her round so violently that she almost lost her balance, that she realised Gareth had been shouting at her.

He shook his head impatiently at her. 'Have you no more sense than to walk about a construction site bareheaded?' he exclaimed, and she saw that he was now wearing a metal helmet for protection. 'Why didn't you stay in the car? You must have known I wouldn't be long!'

He pushed her back towards the station wagon as he spoke, but she protested, turning round to look after her disappointedly. 'I didn't think,' she cried. 'Couldn't I put on a helmet, too?'

Gareth tugged his own off, and slung it into the back of the station wagon. 'Like I said before,' he intoned, getting into the driving seat, 'construction sites are no places for women!'

Caroline stared at him impotently. 'What are you doing? I haven't seen anything yet.'

'You've seen the site,' he remarked mildly. 'That's what you wanted, wasn't it? Besides, there's not much else to see. At the moment, the job's approximately two-thirds completed. We should finish inside six months providing we don't hit any more snags. Right now, we have some problem with subsidence, but I think we can overcome it. Our biggest enemy is a shortage of raw materials. But that's not just a problem here; it's pretty prevalent everywhere.

Even in England.' He rested his elbow on the opened window ledge in his door. 'There: does that give you a reasonably comprehensive rundown of the state of things?'

Caroline put her hands on her hips. 'Do you mean to tell me you've brought me all this way just to take me back again?'

'It was your idea, not mine,' Gareth pointed out dryly.

'Oh—oh, you——' Caroline tried desperately to curb her temper. 'I don't want to go back yet. It's only eleven-thirty!'

Gareth glanced at his wrist watch. 'So it is.' His eyes narrowed. 'So what do you want to do?'

Caroline bent her head, scuffing her sandal in the dusty earth. 'You could show me where you live,' she suggested. 'I'd love a drink of something long and cool.'

Gareth tapped his fingers impatiently on the steering wheel. 'Caroline, I have a job of work to do——'

'It'll be lunch time soon,' she declared. 'Don't tell me you don't stop for lunch, because I won't believe you!'

Gareth studied her a moment longer, and then he said: 'Get in the car!' in uncompromising tones.

Caroline hesitated only seconds before walking round the bonnet and sliding in beside him obediently. She slammed her door with trembling fingers and then sat mutinously in her seat. She wasn't used to being spoken to like that, but his set face had brooked no further argument.

They left the site by the same route as they had reached it, but when they came to a fork in the road, Gareth swung the station wagon abruptly to the left, plunging down steeply through the thick wedge of foreshortened trees and undergrowth. The track was muddy in places and the vehicle slid several yards with ominous speed before Gareth managed to steady their progress again, ploughing over roots and twigs with a strict disregard for the station wagon's suspension.

Caroline would have liked to have asked where he was taking her, but she dared not interrupt his obvious concentration, and she peered about her instead, wondering what his plans were now.

And then she heard a sound which came delightfully to her ears through the open windows. It was the sound of water breaking over stones, a cooling, deliciously inviting sound in the unpleasant heat of the midday sun. She stared ahead in surprise and presently they emerged on to a fern-strewn ledge at the foot of the falls. High overhead, the narrow bridge that crossed the falls could be seen, but they were almost at the foot of the ravine.

Gareth stopped the car and looked at her with a certain amount of exasperation. 'Well,' he said, 'is this more to your liking?'

Caroline clasped her hands together. 'Oh, Gareth, you know it is. It's—marvellous!'

Gareth relaxed in his seat, drawing out a case of cigars and putting one between his teeth. 'I gather Nicolas didn't bring you here,' he remarked, lighting the cigar as he spoke.

'No. Oh, no, we were further down-stream.'

Caroline slid impulsively out of the car and walked to the edge of the ledge, looking down on to a natural stairway of stone that led down to the swirling waters at the foot of the falls. Above, shelves of rock made smooth by the passage of water spread a cascade of turquoise lace. She turned, half thinking that Gareth was beside her, but it was his eyes that she could feel, watching her from the shadows of the car.

Feeling slightly embarrassed, she walked back to him, brushing threads of fern from the flared bottoms of her jeans. As she reached the station wagon Gareth slid out and stretched lazily, his movements attracting her attention as usual.

'I suggest we have our lunch here,' he commented, as his arms fell to his sides. 'Does that appeal to you?'

'Our lunch?' Caroline was taken aback. 'But—but I thought——'

Gareth's expression was slightly sardonic. 'Yes—well, I have to admit that I had no intention of providing you with lunch and what I have will in no way compare to the kind of spread Nick might have provided, but you're welcome to share what I have.'

Caroline flushed. 'I don't understand.'

'It's simple really. My houseboy provides me with a packed lunch when I expect to be out all day, and I find some appropriate spot and eat it. It's as uncomplicated as that.'

'I see.' Caroline made an awkward movement. 'There—there's really no need to rob yourself on my account. I can make do with a drink until I get back home.'

Gareth gave her an old-fashioned look. 'Oh, really? And what am I supposed to do? Sit and eat my lunch while you watch me with those big brown eyes?'

Caroline bent and picked up a broken fern, smoothing it through her fingers. 'I just don't want you to put yourself out on my account!'

'Oh, don't you?' Gareth exhaled smoke into the air above her head. 'And I suppose you being here, at Nyshasa, and not wanting to go home again doesn't put me out!'

Caroline sighed. 'Do you mind? Awfully, I mean?'

Gareth's expression hardened a little. 'If I did, you wouldn't be here,' he retorted, and with that she had to be content.

Gareth's houseboy had provided a more than adequate

lunch for one person. There was half a chicken, some cold baked potatoes, tomatoes and salad, and several crusty rolls. There was also a flask of ice-cold beer, but as there was only one beaker, Gareth drank his from the flask.

Despite Caroline's assertion that she needed only a drink to sustain her, she found herself eating half of the meal that Gareth gave to her with unaccustomed relish. Chicken and salad had never tasted so good, and the rolls were golden brown and mouthwateringly soft beneath their crusty exterior. Even the beer, which hitherto she had always avoided, was cold and refreshing, and infinitely more enjoyable in the open air. They ate their lunch seated on the crumbling bark of some long-dead tree-trunk, keeping a sharp lookout for ants or beetles or any other form of wildlife which might choose to interrupt their meal. Once or twice, Caroline caught Gareth's eyes upon her with a vaguely indulgent expression in their depths, and her heart beat a little more heavily when she considered how achingly attractive he was in this mood. It reminded her of other occasions when they had shared an alfresco meal, and of how once they had had to shelter for hours in an old boat-house by the Thames after being caught by a sudden summer storm.

When they had finished, Gareth gathered all the odds and ends together and took them back to the car, thrusting the cartons and flask into the box on the back seat. Then he came back to where Caroline was sitting, and said:

'Well? What do you want to do now?'

'Are you asking me?' she parried in surprise, slanting a glance up at him through her long lashes.

Gareth flexed his back muscles. 'Don't let's start fencing with one another,' he advised, stifling a yawn. 'I don't work in the midday sun, and no matter what you've heard about mad dogs and Englishmen, quite frankly I'm too tired to play games. I suggest we go back to the car and rest for a while before I take you home.'

Caroline stood up, dusting down the seat of her pants, shivering as an ant detached itself from her leg and dropped to the ground. 'But how can we rest in the car?'

Gareth regarded her patiently. 'There's no problem. You can simply stretch out across the back seat.'

Caroline frowned. 'But what about you?'

'I shall use the front seat. Don't worry—there's plenty of room.'

Caroline lifted her shoulders and then let them fall again. 'But—but won't you be uncomfortable? I mean, you're much taller than I am—and there's the steering wheel to contend with.'

'I hadn't forgotten.' Gareth was sardonic. 'Don't concern yourself. I can manage.'

'But, Gareth——'

'Well, what would you suggest?' he demanded, irritation marring his lean good looks. 'That we share the back? Do you think that would be a good idea? Because I don't!'

Caroline bent her head. 'All right.'

'Right.'

He strode back to the car and scuffling her feet, Caroline followed him.

In spite of her sense of guilt at being given the most comfortable position, Caroline found her eyes drooping almost as soon as her head touched the seat, and she knew nothing more until the shrill squawking of the parakeets which nested in the ravine awakened her to awareness of her surroundings.

Blinking, she raised her wrist to eye level and tried to read the hands of her watch. Amazingly it was after three o'clock and the blazing heat of the day was beginning to yield. She struggled up into a sitting position and then

134

stopped short. Gareth was still sleeping, his long length stretched across the two front seats and out of the car door. He lay on his back, his arms resting just behind his head, his shirt unbuttoned to the waist to reveal the dark tan of his chest and stomach.

Caroline looked down on him, her lips parting tenderly. He looked so much younger in sleep, and there was something slightly covetous about just looking at him without his being aware of it. She had an overwhelming desire to touch him, to lie with him and bring him awake to awareness of her.

Stretching her arm down over the back of the front seat, she slid her fingers under the thin material of his shirt, seeking the warm curve of his shoulder. His skin was smooth, the muscles firm even relaxed like this, and an aching longing for him swept over her so that when he opened his eyes she did not immediately withdraw her hand.

But Gareth was instantly alert to the situation, and he jack-knifed into a sitting position so that she was forced to draw back. 'What the hell do you think you're doing?' he snapped savagely, destroying her mood in seconds.

She stared at him helplessly, hot and embarrassed, and then, needing to get away from his anger, she thrust open the car door and scrambled out. She ran across the clearing to the rocky edge, breathing quickly and jerkily, scarcely able to understand the flooding sweetness of desire which would not be denied. She had never felt this way before, never really comprehended the idea of actually wanting a man. But suddenly everything was plain to her and she ached with a satisfaction denied.

She glanced back at the station wagon. Gareth was still inside. She saw the flare of his lighter as he lit a cigar. Was that all it meant to him? A source of annoyance? An irri-

135

tation that she should dare to touch him without invitation?

And what could she do? There was so little time. One thing was certain, if she went back to England now she could never marry Jeremy Brent. Never at any time had she felt this way about him.

She looked up. The waters of the falls were very inviting to her overheated body. Perhaps it was possible to bathe in the falls. Not at the base where the water swirled so dangerously, but higher up where ledges provided resting places.

Without really stopping to think what she was about to do, she unfastened the belt of her jeans and stepped out of them, tugging her sweater over her head. Then she paddled down the steps to where the first ledge jutted into the cascade. This close a delicious shower of water sprayed her arms and legs and its coolness was very welcoming.

Grasping a handful of the ferny undergrowth which grew close to the outer rocks, she pulled herself on to the lowest ledge and shivered ecstatically as the foamy cascade soaked her through in seconds. In her over-emotional, over-excited state its coldness was doubly chilling, and she waited only a moment before attempting to reach the next ledge up. Perhaps she could climb to the top of the falls this way.

But she had scarcely begun to attempt the second ledge when she heard Gareth's furious voice behind her, yelling: 'For God's sake, Caroline, come back! You'll break your neck if you slip off there!'

Caroline glanced round. Gareth was standing on the rocks where she had abandoned her jeans and sweater, staring up at her frustratedly. A quiver of fear of what he might do to her if she did not obey him rippled through her, but she refused to be treated like a child.

'I'm all right, Gareth,' she called back, shivering in

136

spite of herself. 'Go—go and smoke your cigar! I'll come back when I'm ready!'

'You'll come back now!' he shouted commandingly. 'At once!'

'And if I don't?' She looked round defiantly.

Gareth hesitated only a moment longer and then he unfastened his belt and thrust off his trousers. Underneath, he was wearing navy shorts, and she realised with a sense of dismay that he could come after her if he wanted to. And that apparently was what he intended.

Panic made her careless. Her fingers fumbled hopelessly for a handhold on the ledge above, but it was useless. The stones were smooth and the speed of the water swept away every attempt she made. He was on the ledge below her now, and she looked down into his determined face apprehensively.

'All right, all right!' she cried. 'I'll come back. Just get out of my way.'

Gareth stepped obediently aside and she turned and lowered herself inelegantly over the ledge. But her fingers were wet and the hold she had on the ferns gave way and she screamed as she was swept down by the water.

Then strong hands caught her, preventing her from being dashed down on to the rocks below, and she clung to Gareth weakly, her heart pounding like a drum.

'Oh, I'm sorry—I'm sorry,' she whispered, tears mingling with the water on her cheeks. 'Did I hurt you?'

Gareth said nothing, he merely grasped a firm hold on the rocky ledge and stepped across, hauling her with him. Then he released her and she sank into a trembling little heap at his feet, aware of exactly what he had saved her from.

Gareth stood, legs astride, regarding her grimly, and Caroline looked up at him tremulously. 'I—I've said I'm sorry,' she breathed. 'What more can I say?'

Gareth shook his head angrily. 'Don't say anything.'

'But I must.' She stifled a little sob, sniffing plaintively. 'Don't be angry with me, Gareth—please!'

Gareth looked down at his shorts clinging wetly to his body. 'I think we'd better go back,' he stated coldly.

Caroline caught her lower lip between her teeth. 'Am I such a nuisance, Gareth?' she appealed, stretching out a hand and stroking her fingers down the wet hairs of his leg.

Gareth's eyes darkened and he would have moved abruptly away, but she wrapped her arms possessively round one of his legs, imprisoning it, pressing her face against his skin.

'Oh, Gareth,' she whispered huskily, 'don't be so cruel.'

Gareth bent, his intention to disentangle himself, but it didn't work out like that. When his face was only a few inches from Caroline's she was unable to prevent herself from touching her mouth to his. It was as though that small action was the last straw so far as Gareth was concerned, and he came down beside her, his mouth frankly sensuous, reaching for her with disturbing determination.

He bore her back against the rocky ledge, the weight of his body on hers destroying coherent thought. He cupped her face in his hands, parting her lips with his and seeking the sweetness within. 'Dear God,' he muttered, against her mouth. 'I want you, Caroline.'

Caroline's bare arms curved round his neck, her back arched as he pressed closer, and a low moaning sigh escaped her lips as he lowered his head to find the hollow between her breasts.

'You're beautiful,' he groaned, pressing kisses over her throat and ears and cheeks before returning to her mouth again. 'You always were. But now you're a woman—in

138

every sense of the word.'

Caroline's fingers explored his scalp and the nape of his neck. 'I've missed you so much,' she breathed.

'Have you?' She failed to denote any mockery in his tone. 'I've thought about you, too. Would you believe when I was making love to Sharon I was pretending it was you?'

Caroline caught her breath. 'Sharon? That was your wife?'

'That's right.'

Caroline moved her head helplessly. 'But why did you marry her? Did—did you love her?'

Gareth drew himself upward a little to look down at her. 'What do you think?'

'But—but——' Caroline sought for words. 'It—it was so soon——'

'After us, you mean?' Gareth's lips twisted. 'Yes, well, that's easily explained if you consider the physical aspects of our relationship.'

Caroline's cheeks burned. 'You mean—you mean——'

His eyes had hardened. 'I loved you, Caroline,' he muttered grimly. 'I wanted to marry you. I couldn't take it when you turned me down.'

'Oh, Gareth!' Caroline felt sick. 'Was—was that why your marriage failed?'

He shrugged. 'You might say that. After the—er—image of you faded, my ardour soon cooled. I couldn't blame her when she sought excitement elsewhere.'

'And——' She had to ask the question. 'And—Sandra?'

His face softened. 'Sandra's altogether different.'

Caroline felt the first twinges of anxiety. 'Did you—that is—did your wife suspect that there was—something between you?'

Gareth's eyes darkened again. 'What are you implying?'

139

Caroline wet suddenly dry lips with the tip of her tongue. 'I—I only wondered whether—whether——' She could not go on.

Gareth looked positively furious. 'You wondered whether it was my behaviour—or should I say *mis*behaviour with Sandra that broke up my marriage, is that it?' He sneered. 'Well, no. I'm sorry to disappoint you, but I divorced my wife, not the other way round.'

Caroline's lids hid her eyes. What was happening between them? she asked herself despairingly. She had thought when he kissed her just now that everything was going to be all right—but it wasn't. How could they lie here in each other's arms saying such terrible things to one another? What had gone wrong?

Looking up at him again, she exclaimed: 'Gareth, don't let's hurt one another any more!'

Gareth traced the line of her neck and shoulder with his finger, sliding the strap of her bikini aside to bend his head and caress the soft smooth flesh with his lips. 'I don't think I could hurt you, Caroline,' he spoke indistinctly. 'You're far too aware of your own potential to allow that to happen. But I do want to love you——'

Caroline was no longer yielding. His words had not reassured her at all. In fact she was almost convinced he had every intention of making love to her with or without her consent. What did he think she was? Did he imagine that because she was now a woman she was therefore an emancipated member of the permissive society, allowing any man these kind of intimacies?

She shifted uneasily, her flesh cooling rapidly. What was it he had said? What were the exact words he had used? That he had *loved* her. That was it. The past tense of the verb to love, not the present as she had foolishly imagined. So why was he doing this? What warped objective had he in mind?

'Gareth!' She tried to push him away. 'Let me go!'

Gareth raised his head, a frown drawing his dark brows together. 'Oh, no, Caroline,' he muttered thickly, 'not this time. You won't make a fool of me again!'

Caroline gasped, 'Gareth, you don't understand——'

'I understand very well. I understand that you're a woman now, a woman of experience, a woman free and easy with her favours. And by God, I deserve those favours more than any other man!'

His determination frightened her. For the first time in her life she found herself in a situation she could not control. Her frustrated struggling only seemed to incite him further, and his mouth burned against her chilled body. But desperation found its own weapons and if she could not escape from him by physical means then only words were left to her.

'It seems that living in a uncivilised society for so long has robbed you of your sense of decency—your self-respect!' she gulped between choking breaths. 'What do you think *Sandra* will think about such *primitive* behaviour?'

There was a moment when she thought she had failed, when Gareth continued to kiss her with those long, soul-destroying kisses which even she was not wholly able to resist. But then, as though the mention of Sandra's name in this context drove a wedge between them, he thrust her roughly away from him, lying on his back with an arm across his eyes.

'So you're going to tell Sandra, is that it?' he muttered coldly.

Caroline scrambled to her feet, snatching up her jeans and sweater. So long as he was lying there with his eyes closed she could put some distance between them. She

141

didn't answer his question. She stumbled inelegantly up the stone steps and ran like a wild thing for the comparative safety of the station wagon.

She was dressed and sitting shakily in her seat when he eventually came over the rise, walking with indolent grace towards the car. Even after everything that had happened between them, even knowing the despicable way he regarded her, he still had the power to send the blood coursing more swiftly through her veins and it was terribly difficult not to try once more to appeal to him. Oh, why couldn't he see that she was no wanton, no participant in the sophisticated game of love? She simply loved him, and because of this her response to him was sometimes wild and abandoned.

Gareth didn't say a word. He climbed negligently into the seat beside her and reached for a cigar. Then, when it was lit he started the station wagon's engine and swung it in a semi-circle to make the return journey to the top of the ravine. It was a somewhat hair-raising trip, even more hair-raising than the journey down had been, but Caroline had to sit in silence, her fingers gripping the edge of her seat, praying that if she had to die Gareth would somehow learn the truth about her.

CHAPTER NINE·

THE following morning there was a visitor to the bungalow. It was Helen Barclay, and she arrived when there was no one but Caroline around.

'That's all right, my dear,' she exclaimed, when Caroline hastened to explain that Charles had taken the children to see the mine and that Elizabeth was not up yet. 'It's you I came to see.'

'Me?' Caroline was ungrammatical. Then she smiled. 'Why? Was there some specific reason?'

'As a matter of fact, yes.' Helen indicated Caroline's wrist. 'That bite you had—why didn't you tell me about it straight away?'

'Oh, Helen!' Caroline sighed. 'That was ages ago now. Besides, I was too ashamed. I should have had more sense than to touch the animal.' She frowned. 'Anyway, how do you come to know about it?'

'I'm afraid the grapevine to the Mission works rather more slowly than elsewhere. In fact, I learned about it three days ago—from Gareth, but I've been so busy since then this is the first opportunity I've had to come and apologise.'

At the mention of Gareth's name, Caroline felt herself stiffening, but she managed to say: 'Apologise? There's no need for that.'

'But there is. Gareth's right. I do encourage those beasts, but they always look so thin and starved—I feel sorry for them.'

'Really, Helen, I don't blame you——'

'No. But Gareth does.'

143

Caroline twisted her hands together. 'I'm sure you're mistaken.'

'And is it all right now? You're looking very pale, Caroline. I don't think this climate agrees with you.'

Caroline made a deprecating gesture. 'I'm fine. I—I suppose I shouldn't have been without—without Gareth's help—but——'

'What do you mean?' Helen looked surprised. Then: 'Did you have some—trouble with your arm?'

Caroline flushed. 'I thought Gareth told you.'

'Does it involve him?'

'Yes.'

'Then he wouldn't,' said Helen resignedly. 'But what happened?'

Caroline shook her head. 'Oh, well,' she murmured, reluctantly, 'there was some swelling. It was obviously infected, and as Doctor Macdonald was away, Gareth lanced it himself.'

'I see,' Helen nodded. 'It's just as well you told him about it. He has some small knowledge of such things. He was once bitten by a snake and sucked the poison out himself.'

Caroline was horrified. 'How dreadful!' she breathed, realising with an inward feeling of despair that many such accidents could happen to him out here and she would never know anything about them. He could die—and she would only hear about it indirectly.

She turned away so that Helen should not see the agony in her eyes. 'Er—you'll have some coffee, won't you, Helen?'

'That would be nice.' Helen subsided on to a low chair. 'I told Laurie not to expect me back much before lunch.'

Caroline nodded. 'I'll just tell Thomas.'

But outside in the hall she pressed her burning forehead against the cool plaster of the wall. She felt sick and ill, she had felt this way since her return from Nyshasa yester-day, and the last thing she had expected this morning was to have to entertain a visitor.

When she returned to the living-room she had herself in control again, smiling as Helen admired the orange shift she was wearing.

'You can wear such vivid colours, Caroline,' she ex-claimed. 'Me, I never did look good in bright things. Tell me, have you been getting out and about while you've been here?'

Caroline dug her nails into the soft upholstery of the couch. 'Yes,' she answered steadily, 'we've been to lots of places. Er—Charles and Elizabeth took the children to the Kywari game reserve yesterday.'

'And didn't you go?'

'No. I—er—I was rather tired. I didn't feel like the journey.'

'So you had a day on your own.'

'No. No, actually, I didn't do that either.' Caroline looked up in relief as Thomas brought in the tray. 'Put it here, please,' she indicated the low table in front of her. 'Thank you.'

For a few minutes she busied herself with the coffee, asking Helen whether she wanted sugar, hoping that the older woman would start some new topic of conversation, but when she was comfortably settled with her coffee and a biscuit, Helen said:

'So what did you do yesterday?'

Caroline sighed. 'Well, Gareth came down to bring some medical supplies for Lucas Macdonald, and he—he took me up to see the construction site—where they're building the dam.'

Helen raised her eyebrows. 'I see. And what did you think of it?'

145

'It's very impressive.'

'Hmm.' Helen considered the liquid in her cup. 'It's going to be quite something when it's finished. Nyshasa will be quite civilised in a few years.'

'Yes,' Caroline agreed. This was safe ground and she relaxed a little. But then Helen's next words brought her alert again.

'Do you like Gareth, Caroline?'

'I—he's very nice.' *Nice*! Her stomach plunged. What a description to apply to Gareth.

'Yes.' Helen was unaware of her emotional upheaval. 'Yes, he is nice. I like him enormously. But then everybody likes Gareth. I simply can't understand why his marriage should have ended so disastrously.'

Caroline made a negative sound, feeling that no reply was needed, but Helen went on:

'I think it's such a pity, don't you, that the nicest men get the bitchiest wives?'

'Yes.' Caroline wished they could talk about something else. 'I—I expect it's hard for a young woman—living in Africa.'

'Huh!' Helen snorted. 'It was no harder for her than for any of us.'

Caroline shrugged. 'Well, these things sometimes don't work out.'

'I know, I know.' Helen held out her cup for some more coffee. 'But when you're fond of someone as I am of Gareth, you want to see them happy, and Sharon—that was his wife, you know—she certainly didn't make him happy.'

'I—I don't think it's any concern of mine...' began Caroline uncomfortably, but Helen didn't seem to hear her, or if she did she chose to ignore what she had said.

'Once she said to me that Gareth was to blame—that he'd only married her on the rebound from somebody else

146

—and maybe she was right. But she made little effort to save the marriage. She soon got bored stiff with our lack of amenities, and she'd take herself off to Ashenghi for weeks on end.'

'Helen, *please*—it's nothing to do with me!'

'I know. But it's long past now, and I've no doubt she's having a good time wherever she is. I just feel sorry for Gareth.'

Caroline steadied her cup against her lips with both hands. 'Why should you?' she challenged, rather unevenly.

'I—I mean, he has—Sandra now, doesn't he?'

'Sandra Macdonald?' Helen sounded disgusted. 'You don't suppose she could make a man like Gareth happy, do you?'

'I—I think Gareth—thinks so.'

'What makes you say that?' Helen's eyes were sharp, and Caroline felt the tell-tale colour rising in her cheeks again.

'I—I don't know. I—I just thought that—well, he's often with her, isn't he?'

'Oh, I'm not denying that Sandra would like to think she'll be the next Mrs. Morgan,' said Helen honestly, 'but in that unlikely event I hope they move away. I'd hate to see Gareth disillusioned again.'

Caroline replaced her cup in its saucer. 'Will you have another biscuit?'

Helen shook her head, her eyes suddenly thoughtful. 'Tell me something,' she urged, 'don't you find Gareth attractive? If I were ten years younger, I would.'

Caroline took a deep breath. 'Well—yes. He—he is an attractive man, I'll agree with you there.'

'Then why don't you do something about it?'

Caroline gasped. 'Like what?'

Helen made an impatient gesture. 'I'm sure I don't have

to draw pictures, Caroline. Or does the idea of staying in Africa have no appeal to you either?'

'Helen!' Caroline rose abruptly to her feet. 'You can't organise people's lives for them, you know!'

'I do know that,' remarked Helen quietly, and Caroline turned, contrite.

'Oh, you know I didn't mean—that is, I wasn't referring to your personal affairs, Helen!'

Helen forced a smile. 'No, I'm sure you weren't, Caroline. But nevertheless, you're right. I am an interfering old woman.'

'You're not!' Caroline spread her arms. 'You—you don't understand—certain things, that's all.'

'About you and Gareth?' asked Helen perceptively.

Caroline nodded. 'Yes. About Gareth and me.'

Helen put down her cup and saucer. 'And you don't want to talk about it?'

Caroline shook her head. 'Not really.'

'That's all right——'

'No!' Caroline hesitated. 'No—wait!' It would be a relief to tell somebody, and there was something about Helen that she instinctively liked. 'Actually—actually I knew Gareth years ago.'

Helen listened attentively. 'Before he was married?'

'Yes.' Caroline linked and unlinked her fingers. 'I—I was the girl, you see. The one he wanted to marry.'

'You mean Sharon's story was true? He did marry her on the rebound?'

'Maybe.' Caroline was cautious.

'And did you know he was here when you came?'

'Yes.'

'Did he know you were coming?'

'Not from me. But he learned indirectly through Nicolas.'

148

'I see.' Helen shook her head in a perplexed manner. 'Then—what has happened? If you knew he would be here you must have wanted to see him.'

'I did.' Caroline's voice wobbled. 'Oh, Helen, I—I love him! I thought—I hoped that he might still love me!'

'And he doesn't?'

'No.'

'How can you be sure?'

'Oh, I'm sure.' Caroline nodded her head over and over again.

Helen sighed. 'What a situation!'

'Yes, isn't it?' Caroline paced restlessly about the room. 'Well, now you know.'

Helen followed her progress thoughtfully. 'But are you sure about this, Caroline? Sure that you love him—and that he doesn't love you? I mean, it must be several years since you've seen him. What if you were motivated by a desire to recreate something that—well, has magnified itself out of all proportion in your mind? Maybe the fact that you're not married—or engaged——'

Caroline swung round on her. 'You're implying that I'm desperate for a husband, aren't you? In the politest possible way? Oh, don't deny it! Gareth's already accused me of that in a much less courteous manner!'

'Caroline—my dear——'

'Well, it's the truth. That is what you're saying. But it's not like that!' Caroline pressed her palms together. 'I don't know whether you'll believe this, but before I left England I was engaged—engaged to a man who has everything—looks, a good job, plenty of money—but whom I didn't love! Oh, we've been engaged for a while, and he wanted us to get married. There was no reason why we shouldn't. We had none of the usual problems of lack of funds or accommodation. Jeremy has three homes—plus a villa in the South of France.' She heaved a sigh. 'So what are you thinking now? That he turned me down? That he jilted me?' She shook her head. 'You couldn't be more wrong. He—he's crazy about me.' Her voice broke. 'But— but I found that Gareth was no longer married—that he and his wife were divorced—and—and I couldn't go on with my engagement.'

Helen stood up and caught the younger girl's hands. 'Oh, Caroline!' she exclaimed helplessly.

Caroline tried to compose herself. 'Yes, farcical, isn't it? Jeremy loves Caroline, Caroline loves Gareth, and Gareth loves someone else!'

Helen shook her head. 'I doubt very much whether it's as simple as that. These things never are. Have you told Gareth about this man in England, this Jeremy?'

'No, of course not.'

'Why—of course not?'

'Helen, whenever—whenever Gareth and I have been together, our conversations haven't exactly been cordial. Besides, it's no use. I know exactly what Gareth feels for me, and it isn't love.'

Helen released her hands to move regretfully to the window. 'I'm sorry.'

'Yes, so am I.'

There was silence for a few moments and then, unexpectedly, there was a knock at the outer door. Caroline frowned, rubbing her palms vigorously against her cheeks to hide any tell-tale signs of emotion. Who could be calling at this hour of the morning? The only person she could think of was Nicolas, and with a helpless look at Helen she went to answer the door.

But it wasn't Nicolas. It was Sandra Macdonald, and she looked beyond Caroline into the hall, saying: 'Hello. May I come in?'

Caroline was taken aback, but she stepped back at once. 'Of course. What can I do for you?'

Sandra looked into the lounge, not immediately noticing Helen by the window. 'We'll go in here.' Then: 'Oh, hello, Helen! I didn't realise you were here.'

Helen half smiled. 'I'm just leaving, Sandra.'

Caroline looked from one to the other of them. 'Oh, please,' she appealed to the older woman. 'Don't go! I—I was going to ask whether you'd like to stay for lunch.'

'I'd love to, Caroline, but I'm afraid Laurie wouldn't be very pleased if I wasn't home to prepare something for him. No, I must go, thanks all the same, Caroline.' She smiled encouragingly at her. 'I've enjoyed our little chat. You must come over to the mission again before you leave.'

'I'd like that.'

Excusing herself for a moment, Caroline accompanied Helen to the door, and after she had waved her off she returned to the living room.

'Charles has taken the children to the mine,' she remarked, gathering the empty coffee cups together. 'But I shouldn't think Elizabeth will be long.'

'That's all right.' Sandra's smile was thin. 'I can wait.' She seated herself on the couch. 'I didn't realise you knew Helen Barclay so well.'

Caroline looked up from her task. 'Oh, we don't know one another that well. It's just that we seem to hit it off together, that's all.'

Sandra nodded. 'Oh, I see.'

Caroline lifted the tray. 'Er—would you like some coffee?' She had to be hospitable even if Sandra's attitude was somewhat less than friendly. She didn't know what it was, but Sandra had a definite look of hostility about her.

Sandra hesitated, then she nodded. 'Why not?' She

glanced round. 'Where is Elizabeth, anyway?'

Caroline walked to the door. 'I expect she's getting dressed now. She didn't hurry up this morning when Charles was taking the children out.' She omitted the fact that Elizabeth didn't hurry up *any* morning.

'I see.'

Sandra nodded and Caroline left her to ask Thomas for more coffee. When she returned, Sandra was flicking impatiently through the pages of a magazine.

'You have it pretty easy, here, don't you?' she challenged, as Caroline came into the room.

Caroline was taken aback. 'I—well, if you say so.'

'I do.' Sandra thrust the magazine aside, her eyes hard and accusing. 'I mean, you're pretty familiar with your employers, aren't you? And they seem to go out of their way to be considerate towards you.'

'We get along very well, if that's what you mean.'

'That's not exactly what I mean, and you know it. I've noticed that in this household you're treated more as a friend than a nanny.'

'I'm not really a nanny,' pointed out Caroline mildly. 'I agreed to come out here to help Elizabeth with the children, that's all. My real occupation is schoolteaching.'

Sandra frowned. 'Then what are you doing playing at being a nanny?'

Caroline curbed the desire to tell Sandra that it was no business of hers really, and replied: 'Elizabeth asked me to come, and I—I found the idea very interesting——'

'Not least because you knew Gareth Morgan was here, I suppose,' snapped Sandra.

Caroline felt as though someone had hit her in the stomach. 'I—I don't know what you mean——'

'Oh, yes, you do.' Sandra glared at her. 'I know you came here to see Gareth. He told me.'

'He—told—you——' Caroline couldn't take it in.

'Yes,' Sandra sneered. 'I don't know how you had the nerve to do it! Come here, I mean. You've made things very awkward for Gareth.'

Caroline felt faint. 'I—don't see that——'

'No, you wouldn't. You're only interested in your own selfish ends.'

Thomas came in with the coffee, smiling pleasantly at them both, but Caroline couldn't respond. She felt sick to her stomach, and her pale cheeks must have communicated her condition to Thomas, because he said: 'You feeling all right, miss?'

Caroline managed to nod. 'Yes. Yes, I'm fine, thank you, Thomas. Just put the tray here, as before.'

After the houseboy had gone, Sandra eyed her companion critically. 'I must say you do look pretty sick!' she observed, without sympathy. 'But it's time somebody told you a few home truths!'

'So you took it upon yourself to do it, is that right, Sandra?' Caroline asked, forcing a calmness she did not feel.

'Someone had to,' retorted Sandra scornfully. 'It's rather pathetic really, were it not so damned insolent!'

Caroline tackled the coffee cups automatically, wincing when the pot clattered against a rim, almost upsetting the liquid. She pushed a cup towards Sandra, wondering how one could continue to perform such mundane tasks when the person opposite was mentally annihilating you. Then she rose to her feet.

'If you'll excuse me, I'll tell Elizabeth you're here.'

Sandra looked up. 'Just one more thing, Caroline. Two days ago Gareth asked me to marry him. I accepted. So keep away from him in future, will you? He's simply not interested.'

Caroline turned away, unable to say another word, walking blindly out of the room. She heard movements in Elizabeth's bedroom, but she didn't attempt to speak to her. She walked unseeingly to her own room, and then flung herself on the bed, aching sobs racking her body. Let Elizabeth find Sandra waiting for her. She didn't care how long the other girl might have to wait.

CHAPTER TEN

By the following day, Caroline had achieved a rather precarious form of composure. There was no point in pretending any longer that Gareth might change his mind about her, and the sooner she accepted this fact the easier it would be. Besides, he was now engaged to Sandra, and was as inaccessible as he had ever been. She would simply have to wait out the days until they returned to England and then resume her life as though this period in time had never happened. But the constant dull pain in her stomach could not be dismissed so easily, and the heavy ache near her heart might become a permanent fixture. Only one certain thing had come out of all this. It would not be fair to her to marry Jeremy feeling as she did about Gareth. She would never be sure that should Gareth ever come back into her life, she would be able to prevent herself from going to him in the unlikely event of his wanting her to.

It was fortunate that Charles and Elizabeth should choose this particular day to have another of their periodic rows. Charles had promised to take Elizabeth and the children to Nicolas Freeleng's for lunch, but a sudden emergency at the mine had necessitated his presence there and Elizabeth had refused to go alone. They had argued violently for several minutes and then Charles had stalked off saying he would get someone to give him a lift to the mine so that if Elizabeth should change her mind the car would be available to her.

After he had gone, Elizabeth had locked herself in the bedroom and Caroline was left with the children. Not

155

that she objected. Charles and Elizabeth's absorbtion with their own affairs had prevented them from noticing how pale and heavy-eyed she was looking, and she was glad of the children's company to help banish her depression.

'What shall we do?' she asked brightly, as David and Miranda were moping about the living room. 'Would you like to go for a walk?'

Miranda sniffed. 'Why do Mummy and Daddy have such awful rows?' she asked tearfully. 'Do all mummies and daddies have rows?'

Caroline sighed. 'I expect there are occasions when everyone loses their temper,' she comforted. 'You'll see. Daddy will come home this afternoon and everything will be fine.'

'Yes, but we won't get to go to Mr. Freeleng's, will we?' demanded David moodily. 'I like going there, and that's why Mummy got so angry—because Daddy wouldn't take us.'

'Daddy had an urgent job to do at the mine,' said Caroline firmly. 'He couldn't neglect his job to take you to Nyshasa.'

'Huh!' David scuffed his toe. 'Well, now we can't go at all. Mummy won't take us.'

Caroline bit her lip. 'Well, the car's outside. I suppose we could go for a drive, if you like.'

David's eyes widened. 'To Nyshasa?'

'No—no, not that far.' Caroline tried to ignore his disappointed face. 'I meant—well, just a drive. Wouldn't you like that, Miranda?'

Miranda hesitated. 'I s'pose we could. But where could we go?'

Caroline considered the question. 'We could go to the Mission,' she suggested.

'That's only a tiny distance,' returned David scornfully.

'Why can't we go to Nyshasa?'

'Because I don't intend to drive that far!' stated Caroline, half impatiently. She was beginning to wish she had never suggested using the car. 'Don't you think you're being rather unreasonable? I mean—I might have expected us to just stay here.'

David shrugged. 'Well, I'd rather do that than go to the Mission,' he declared.

'Why?' Caroline stared at him. 'I thought you liked playing with the children there.'

'It was all right.' David was evidently set on going to Nyshasa and nothing would budge him. 'But I don't want to go there again.'

'Then we'll just have to stay here,' said Caroline, flopping down into an armchair. 'It's too hot to argue.'

Miranda's lips quivered. 'I didn't say I didn't want to go to the Mission,' she exclaimed.

Caroline sighed. 'Miranda darling, we can't go to the Mission and leave David here—not when Mummy's not available.'

'I could go to Sandra's,' said David, at once. 'I like going there. Besides,' he brightened considerably, 'Gareth might be there and he might take us out with him. I'd like that.'

'I doubt very much whether Gareth will be down in La Vache this morning,' retorted Caroline dampeningly, trying to bear the agonising shaft of jealousy that tore through her without flinching.

'Why? He might be.' David was indignant. 'Anyway, that's what I'd rather do.'

Caroline shook her head. 'David, you can't simply go and wish yourself on—on Sandra.'

'Why not? She said I could go there—any time!'

Miranda wrinkled her small nose. 'Well, I don't want

157

to go to Sandra's. I'd rather go to the Mission with Caroline.'

Caroline got to her feet. 'Look, this is silly. David, you'll have to come with us.'

David clenched his small fists. 'Why? Why should I? You can't make me.'

'I have no intention of making you, as you put it. It's simply that—well, Sandra probably has things to do.'

'But can't I ask her?' David changed his tactics. 'Can't I? I mean, she only has to say yes or no.'

Caroline hesitated. 'You'd better ask your mother first.'

David hunched his shoulders. 'Oh, can't you do that, Caroline? She'll only get angry if I go to her door.'

Caroline thrust her hands into the waistline pockets of her jeans. 'Oh, all right, I'll ask her. But if she says no you'll have to come with us.'

'All right,' David nodded.

Much against her better judgement, Caroline knocked at Elizabeth's door. There was no immediate answer, and with lowering spirits she knocked again.

There was silence for a moment, and then Elizabeth's petulant voice called: 'Who is it? What do you want?'

'It's me! Caroline!'

'Oh, you'd better come in, then.' Elizabeth could be heard sliding out of bed and pattering to the door on bare feet to unlock it. 'What is it?' she demanded. 'Has something happened?' She looked beyond Caroline hopefully. 'Has Charles come back?'

'No. No, it's nothing like that, Elizabeth.' Caroline licked her lips. 'I've offered to take the children to the Mission in the car, but David doesn't want to go——'

'He can't stay here with me——'

'I know that.' Caroline ignored Elizabeth's selfishness. 'He wants to go and ask Sandra if he can remain with her.

Would you mind if he did?'

'What? Ask Sandra Macdonald if he can stay there?' Elizabeth considered. 'I don't see why not. Why? Do you have any objections?'

Caroline flushed. 'No, of course not. So long as you're agreeable, it's all right with me.'

'Good.' Elizabeth looked pointedly back towards the bed. 'Is that all?'

'Yes, that's all,' Caroline nodded. 'Sorry to have disturbed you.'

Elizabeth caught a trace of sarcasm in her voice. 'There's no need to be like that, Caroline. I know you think I'm behaving childishly, but this has been a pretty rotten holiday so far, and I for one shall be glad to go home.'

'I see.' Caroline half turned away.

'Actually, I'm thinking of going sooner than I expected,' went on Elizabeth. 'You might as well know, I think a month is quite long enough to expect us to stay in these conditions.'

'But that means we'll be leaving in less than a week!' Caroline was horrified.

'That's right,' Elizabeth nodded. 'You think about it, Caroline, and if you're enjoying yourself, make the most of it while you can.'

Caroline walked back to the lounge feeling numb and strangely bereft. Although she had thought she had resigned herself to returning to England and giving up all thoughts of seeing Gareth again, now that the opportunity presented itself the enormity of what it meant to her was frightening. It was one thing to consider leaving in the light of several more weeks before the day came, and quite another to consider returning to England in only a few days.

Sandra Macdonald saw the car as soon as it stopped near

their bungalow. She was at the front of the building, tending some plants she had obviously cultivated, but she came down the path to the road looking at Caroline with scarcely concealed dislike. However, when David jumped out of the vehicle her expression changed.

'Hello, David,' she greeted him warmly. 'Have you come to see me?'

'Actually,' said Caroline, choosing her words carefully, 'Miranda and I are going to the Mission and David doesn't want to join us. He'd like to stay with you instead. Would you mind?'

Sandra's eyes narrowed for a moment, and then she looked down at the small boy. 'You want to stay with me, David?' she asked, with apparent satisfaction. 'Then of course you can.'

David whooped with excitement. 'See, Caroline!' he enthused boastfully, 'I told you Sandra wouldn't mind.'

'Did—Caroline think I would?' Sandra spoke to the child.

'Well, she didn't want to ask you——' began David, when Caroline intervened.

'The word was bother, David,' she stated impatiently. 'I said not to bother—Sandra.'

'It's no bother.' Sandra turned to her. 'And it will be easier for you with just Miranda, won't it?'

Her meaning was evident, and Caroline's fingers were taut about the wheel. 'I'll be back about one o'clock,' she said briefly.

'There's no need,' returned Sandra, patting David's head. 'We can have lunch together. There's no need for you to hurry back on David's account.'

Caroline put the car into gear. 'Thank you,' she said, between clenched teeth, and drove away.

Helen and Laurie Barclay were delighted to see them and

160

when they discovered that Caroline had no reason for hurrying back they insisted that they stayed for lunch. Miranda was quite happy to potter around after Helen, and when Helen made some pastry for lunch and gave Miranda a little to work with, she was in seventh heaven. She eventually produced a peach pie which everyone had to have a taste of and clearly enjoyed being the centre of attraction in David's absence.

Caroline drove back to La Vache in the late afternoon. It had been an unusually pleasant day in spite of this morning's unpleasantness, and she thought that Helen Barclay would be one person she would miss when she got back to England.

She stopped at the Macdonalds' bungalow and directing Miranda to remain in the car she walked up the path to the door. Sandra answered the door, her eyes cool and calculating. 'Yes?'

Caroline frowned. 'I've called for David,' she said.

'David?' Sandra moved her shoulders dismissingly. 'He's not here.'

'Not here?' Caroline couldn't take it in. 'Then where is he?'

'He went home just after lunch.'

Caroline was annoyed. 'But you said I had no need to hurry back. That David could stay here as long as he liked——'

'He wanted to go home, so he went.' Sandra was indifferent.

'But you knew I expected him to stay here!' Caroline exclaimed frustratedly. Then: 'Thank you!' and she marched back to the car.

'Where's David?' asked Miranda in surprise as she got in.

'He's gone home,' answered Caroline shortly, and stalled

161

the car in her annoyance.

Thomas was in the living-room when Caroline entered the bungalow and he nodded smilingly to her, a gesture which she was not in the mood to appreciate. But before she could say anything, he said: 'Massa Lacey, he said to tell you that he and Mrs. Lacey have gone to Luanga, Miss Caroline.'

Caroline's heart almost stopped beating. 'Charles and Elizabeth have gone to Luanga,' she echoed. 'Then where's David?'

'David?' Thomas shook his head. 'David with you.'

'No.' Caroline shook her head. 'No, David's not with me. He came home.'

'From the Mission?' Thomas was clearly mystified.

'No.' Caroline tried to remain calm. 'No, Thomas, not from the Mission. He stayed with Miss Macdonald—Sandra Macdonald, you know?—and he left there and came home here soon after lunch. Haven't you seen him?'

Thomas shook his head. 'No, sir.'

'Oh, God!' Caroline's head pounded. 'Look, Thomas, are you sure?'

'Yes, miss. He never came here.'

Miranda started to cry. 'David's lost,' she sobbed.

'Oh, don't be silly, Miranda,' exclaimed Caroline, unnecessarily brusque. 'Of course he's not lost!' But she was less than confident of that fact. 'He must have gone somewhere else.' *But where*?

Trying to think calmly, Caroline took Thomas back over everything that had happened with deliberate slowness, trying to establish some clue to David's whereabouts.

'Could he possibly have gone with Charles and Elizabeth?' she asked, and then answered herself by shaking her head. If he had either Thomas or Sandra would have known about it.

162

Sandra! Caroline walked to the door. Perhaps she might be able to shed some light on to his whereabouts. She recalled David once telling her about two boys who lived near Sandra. Could he possibly have gone there? And if he had, wouldn't their parents have made some attempt to inform the Laceys of their son's whereabouts?

But Sandra was in the shower, informed the houseboy, when Caroline again knocked at the Macdonalds' door and she turned away frustratedly. The shadows of evening were beginning to cast pools of darkness beneath the trees, and with the sinking of the sun darkness would fall like a cloak over the settlement. David had to be located before then, or any manner of accident might befall him.

Caroline returned to the bungalow where Thomas was waiting with Miranda, unaccountably chilled by a sudden thought that had occurred to her. She was recalling David's disappointment at not going to Nyshasa. Surely he couldn't have got bored at Sandra's and decided to try and reach the river on foot, could he? The idea wasn't feasible, it wasn't reasonable, but it was—possible.

'Thomas,' she said at last, 'I want you to remain here with Miranda while I take the car and have a good look round for David. He's sure to be somewhere close by. He may even be hiding to give us a fright. So if you're here, you'll be able to deal with anything that happens, won't you?'

Miranda started to cry again. 'I don't want to stay with Thomas, Caroline, I want to come with you.'

'Darling, you can't.' Caroline dared not suggest to the little girl that her brother might have been foolhardy enough to venture away from the settlement alone. 'Don't you see? I need you to stay here with Thomas to explain to Mummy and Daddy if they should get back before me.'

Miranda rubbed her knuckles over her eyes. 'I don't

163

want to stay here,' she repeated. 'I want to come and find David.'

'And what if David's here all the time?' Caroline tried to tease her. 'What will he think if you go looking for him? Do you want him to laugh at you for being a scaredy-cat?'

Miranda looked a little brighter. 'You think he might only be playing a game?'

'I—not exactly. I said he might be.' Caroline sighed and looked at Thomas. 'You'll do as I say?'

'Yes, miss.' Thomas's amiable face was reassuring.

Outside, it was much darker, and Caroline switched on the car's headlights before moving away from the bungalow. She was acting automatically, refusing to allow blind panic to govern her actions. Panicking would help no one, least of all David, but it was hard to accept the thought of him wandering somewhere in the jungle, at the mercy of every snake and predator the area had to offer.

There were lights in a bungalow near Sandra's and on impulse Caroline went to the door. The woman who answered was slim and attractive, and two small boys stuggled to get past her as she asked what Caroline wanted. This obviously was the mother of the boys David had talked about, but unhappily she had no information to give her.

'He was here earlier,' she volunteered. 'He told Joseph he was having lunch with Sandra.'

'Yes. Yes, he did.' Caroline swallowed her disappointment. 'Well, thank you very much. I'm sorry to have troubled you.'

'Oh, not at all.' The woman looked concerned. 'As soon as my husband comes home I'll have him institute a search if you haven't found him by then.'

'That's very kind of you.' Caroline managed a faint smile. 'I'll let you know if I have any luck.'

It was quite dark by the time she had circled the

settlement and only the roads beyond left any hope. She knew he was not likely to turn in the direction of the Mission, therefore he had to have set off for Nyshasa.

She drove slowly, stopping the car every now and then to get out and shout: '*David!*' at the top of her voice. But apart from the raucous protest of some night animal, there was no answer to her appeals. In addition to which it started to rain, huge globules of water which spattered on to her bare arms, reminding her that it was much cooler now and she had not brought a jacket. Even so, her own personal comfort was of so much less importance than David's that she paid little attention to the fact that her continual sallies into the wet were soaking her to the skin.

The road seemed so much less navigable at night, dark and unfamiliar, without even the comfort of cat's eyes to keep her in a steady course. Eyes did wink at her from the sides of the road, but she tried to pay no attention to them, refusing to speculate what their owners might be. Monkeys, probably, or deer, she consoled herself, dismissing the possibility that such timid animals probably did not venture out at night.

The rain came down more heavily and the windscreen wipers had to work at full pressure to keep the steady stream of water from blocking her vision completely. It would have been easier to walk, she thought, but she had no coat or covering of any kind, and it would be crazy to leave the station wagon and possibly lose her way altogether. She had no torch, no light other than the headlights, and they were not brilliant in this kind of weather.

She wondered where David could be, anxiety finally surfacing in spite of her determination not to give in to it. How could he have been foolish enough to leave the settlement? His father would be so angry, and she dared not think how Elizabeth would react. It was her own fault, of course. She should have insisted that David came with her to the Mission, or if not made sure that she was back in case something like this happened. But how was she to know that Charles would succumb to his wife's urgings and come back to take her out leaving the bungalow unattended. Except for Thomas ...

She frowned. Thomas had said that he hadn't seen him, so that meant that David hadn't gone back to the bungalow at all. But Sandra had said he left just after lunch ... Caroline put a hand to her head. Surely Sandra wouldn't have allowed him to leave her without making sure he went home? Surely that was her responsibility? Besides, David liked her, he liked playing with the boys next door. Why had he left the bungalow in the first place?

It was all confusing, but one thing was emerging from the rest—she was wasting her time going any farther. She had already covered more than five miles. David could not have got any farther, not without help, and sticking to the road as she was, she would never find him if he was in difficulties elsewhere. But what could she do? It was raining so hard, there was no moon, and she had shouted herself hoarse.

Bringing the station wagon to a halt, she looked around. The jungle closed about her, dark and menacing and she shivered. She would have to go back. That was all she could do. She must just pray to God that it had all been some terrible mistake and that David was safely back home.

She swung the steering wheel round to its farthest point and then put the vehicle into reverse. The station wagon skidded backward, responding to her acceleration, and with swift movements she thrust it forward into first gear, swinging the wheel quickly back in the opposite direction. The station wagon started forward at a rush, but she was afraid that if she was hesitant, the wheels would skid on the muddy surface of the road and she would be stuck. As it was, the front wheels went out of control, sliding sideways, and although she fought desperately to right them, it was no good. The acceleration she was using drove her forward and sideways, and with a terrifying speed the nearside wheels encountered the sliding edge of a ditch. The weight of the station wagon propelled it down and Caroline was trying helplessly to keep the vehicle upright when its wheels encountered the spreading roots of a baobab tree and stopped dead. Caroline was thrown forward, her head encountered the steering wheel, and she knew no more.

CHAPTER ELEVEN

CAROLINE came round reluctantly, blinking in the light of a lantern suspended somewhere close at hand. She was aware of hands running in an exploratory fashion over her body, smoothing the thick weight of her hair from her face, wiping her forehead with something cold and wet. There was a voice, too. A strangely familiar, yet unfamiliar voice, murmuring her name over and over again in a curiously agonised fashion: 'Caroline! Caroline, for God's sake, speak to me!'

Her eyes flickered open and she stared uncomprehendingly at Gareth, kneeling on the seat beside her, his face pale and drawn, his eyes dark and glittering.

'Gareth,' she managed unsteadily. 'Wh—what happened?'

'Oh, God, Caroline!' he muttered, with obvious relief, 'I thought I wasn't going to be able to bring you round.'

Caroline moved her head slightly and was immediately conscious of a distinct throbbing in her temple. She put a dazed hand to her forehead, trying to think, and her fingers came away stained with blood. She looked down at the redness without consciously realising it was her own blood, and Gareth uttered an imprecation and gently wiped her forehead again with his handkerchief.

His nearness was reassuring somehow and for a few moments she closed her eyes again and tried to remember what had happened. What was Gareth doing here? Why was he being so kind to her? What had precipitated this sudden show of concern?

'Caroline!' He was speaking to her again, and her eyes

flickered open. 'How do you feel?'

She moved her shoulders. 'I'm in the station wagon,' she said confusedly. 'Why is it all tipped over on one side?'

Gareth laid a hand against her neck, and she could feel he was trembling. 'Don't you remember?'

And suddenly she did! She remembered that David was missing, that he was lost somewhere in this desolate, rain-washed jungle, and she had been trying to find him.

'David——' she began, and she saw Gareth's eyes mirror his relief.

'David's fine,' he assured her. 'He was never missing.'

'But——'

'He went to Luanga with his mother and father.'

'Oh, thank God!' Caroline struggled into a sitting position as best she could on the sloping seat of the vehicle. Then: 'But what are you doing here? How did you know where I was?'

Gareth withdrew his hand from her neck. 'I've been looking for you,' he muttered shortly. 'Do you think you can lever yourself across the seat so that I can get you out and into my car? You're cold and wet, and the sooner I get you back to the bungalow the better.'

Caroline drew a trembling breath. 'I'm afraid I had a bit of an accident,' she offered, attempting a lightness she did not feel. She touched her head again, recognising the blood for what it was. 'Have I cut my head?'

'It's not much more than a scratch,' he replied, backing out of the station wagon and climbing down into the ditch. 'Head wounds always bleed a lot. It's almost stopped anyway. You had a pretty hefty bump on the steering wheel. It's a blessing you didn't go through the windscreen instead. You could have cut your throat!'

Caroline tried to smile. 'That would have saved you the trouble, wouldn't it, Gareth?' she attempted tremulously, but he did not seem to find it amusing.

She struggled after him, grasping the frame of the door to lever herself to the edge of the passenger seat. The door at her side was successfully jammed against the side of the ditch. Gareth waited until he could get both hands to her, and then he lifted her bodily out of the vehicle and carried her up the bank to stand her on her feet on the rough surface of the road. The rain was still coming down in torrents and she swayed as he turned to lock up the vehicle as best he could. Muttering an exclamation, he did what he had to do and then came back to her, the lantern he had used in his hand.

'Couldn't you have got into my car?' he demanded harshly, indicating its dim outline at the other side of the road.

Caroline caught her breath. 'I—I didn't think,' she murmured, shivering.

Gareth took her elbow and urged her across the road to his own station wagon, flinging open the door and reaching inside. 'There's a rug here,' he said. 'I suggest you strip off those wet things and put it round you.'

Caroline looked down at her bedraggled shirt and shorts. 'I—I——' she began.

'I'll look the other way,' muttered Gareth dryly, and slid across into his own seat.

Caroline hesitated only a moment before doing as he suggested and stripping off her wet clothes. Then she gathered the folds of the rug around her, and slid carefully into the passenger seat. 'There—I've done it,' she murmured, beginning to feel the unaccustomed warmth spreading deliciously all over her body.

Gareth turned from his contemplation of the hedgerow and surveyed her thoughtfully, switching on the interior light to have a better look at her head. He flicked the hair aside with a careless finger, leaning closer to her as he did so, and she looked up at him with wide appealing eyes.

'I—I suppose I have to thank you yet again,' she breathed huskily. 'How—how did you know where to find me?'

'I didn't.' He drew back uncompromisingly. 'I was simply one of the search party.'

'Search party?' she echoed weakly. 'For—for me?'

'Of course.' He frowned impatiently. 'Haven't you any idea what time it is?'

'No.' She shook her head, looking down at her wrist just emerging from the folds of the rug. 'My watch has stopped. What time is it?'

Gareth held his wrist out for her to see and she gasped. 'Half past eleven! It can't be!'

'I assure you it is. Just tell me one thing: what were you doing on this road?'

Caroline frowned now. 'I thought David had set off to walk to Nyshasa.'

'You think this is the road to Nyshasa?'

'Isn't it?'

'No. You left the main road a couple of miles back. This road leads nowhere. Except to the swamp.'

'The swamp?' she echoed faintly. 'What swamp?'

'It doesn't have a name. It's what the Africans call black water. God——' He seemed unable to go on for a moment. 'Do you realise if you'd continued along this road——'

He clenched his fists, resting them on the steering wheel. 'Well——' he gathered his composure, 'that's not important now. What is important is getting you back to the Laceys' as quickly as possible. You see, there's someone there waiting to see you.'

Caroline stared at his profile. 'Waiting to see me? Who?'

Gareth gave her a sideways glance. 'He says he's your

171

fiancé. Is he?'

Caroline pressed her fingertips to her lips. 'Not——
Jeremy!'

'Jeremy Brent. That was his name as far as I remember.'

'Dear heaven!' Caroline couldn't take it in. 'But what's
he doing here?'

Gareth's eyes were cold and calculating. 'As I said—
he says he's your fiancé.'

'He's not!' The words broke out of her. 'We—we were
engaged, but—but I broke it off.'

Gareth half turned in his seat towards her. 'Why?'

Caroline looked him squarely in the eyes. 'Do you really
want to know?'

'I shouldn't have asked otherwise.' Gareth had a pulse
working rapidly low on his jawline.

'Well,' she bent her head, 'well, because I—found out
that you—were divorced.'

Gareth's arm was along the back of her seat and his
fingers dug tortuously into the leather. 'Why should that
matter to you?'

Caroline stared at him. 'You know why!'

Gareth's mouth worked savagely. 'I only know that you
threw me over because you wanted to marry some damn
accountant with an eye to the main chance. So here's your
opportunity. Why aren't you taking it? I know enough of
London to appreciate what being headmaster of a school
like Brent's means.'

Caroline gathered the rug more closely about her, although heat was warming her body now from the inside
out. 'If—if you hadn't married—Sharon, we—we might
have been married——' she whispered.

'What do you mean?'

'Within six months I—I had realised my mistake—and
I wanted to come back to you. But—but you were already

172

married to Sharon, and several thousand miles out of reach.'

'Do you expect me to believe that?' Gareth's face was grim.

'It's the truth!' she declared passionately. 'Like you said, my mother influenced me. I was young, and foolish. It took me a little time to realise how wrong she was. Oh, Gareth, you've no idea what it was like for me, thinking of you with another woman——' Her voice broke and as though the sound penetrated the shell he had built around himself all these years, he reached for her, drawing her determinedly against him, burying his face in the warm softness of her neck.

'Caroline, Caroline, Caroline,' he groaned, over and over again. 'Do you want to drive me out of my mind?'

His mouth sought and found hers in a wholly satisfying way, his arms sliding beneath the rug to hold her more firmly against him. 'And what are you trying to say,' he muttered, against the warm curve of her breast, 'that you want to marry me now?'

'Are you asking me?' she breathed, and he nodded, continuing to kiss her.

'Yes, I'm asking you—or telling you—or agreeing to whatever you want,' he said, rather thickly. 'I can't let you go now, no matter what anyone says, and if you do try to leave me again I'll come after you and—well, I'm sure you know what I mean.'

Caroline shivered with ecstatic expectation. There was no possible chance of her wanting to leave Gareth ever again. He was her man, the one man she had ever loved, the years had at least proved that.

But as though her shiver had brought him to his senses, Gareth very reluctantly drew away from her, trapping her hands that would have reached for him again inside the rug and folding it closely about her.

173

'No,' he murmured huskily, 'we've got to get back. We've got to let everyone know that you're all right. Personally, I can think of nothing more desirable than remaining here with you, but my personal desires will have to wait—at least for a while,' he added, his eyes disturbingly sensuous as they rested on her flushed cheeks.

Then he switched out the light and determinedly started the engine. Caroline gave a deep sigh and turned so that she could see his profile. 'Tell me,' she murmured, 'tell me you love me!'

'I love you!' he muttered, keeping his hands on the wheel with an obvious effort. 'Caroline, please! I'm only human, and right now I'd like to——' He broke off. 'What about this man Brent? What are you going to tell him?'

'Whatever you like, darling,' she tantalised. 'You tell him—tell him you're going to marry me.'

Gareth glanced at her. 'Shall I do that?'

His words sobered her. Of course she couldn't let Gareth do it. It was her duty. She would have to tell Jeremy herself.

'No,' she said at last. 'I'll tell him. Poor Jeremy! What a wasted journey!'

She snuggled closer against Gareth and he looked down at her, naked desire smouldering in his eyes. 'Caroline, do you know what you're doing to me?' he demanded.

She coloured and moved a little away from him and as she did so, something else occurred to her. 'David! You said he was with Charles and Elizabeth?'

'That's right.'

'But—but how? Thomas said he didn't come back to the house.'

'He didn't.'

'But——'

'They picked him up at Sandra's.'

174

A cold finger touched Caroline's stomach. Until this moment she had forgotten Sandra. But how could she have done that? She had said that Gareth had asked *her* to marry him. That they were *engaged*! Oh, God, it couldn't be true. Not now.

Swallowing, she said: 'At—at Sandra's? But—but she said——'

'Yes? What did she say?'

Caroline shook her head. Oh, no, she thought. Not now. They couldn't have an argument about Sandra now. 'Nothing,' she managed unsteadily. 'Is—is it much farther?'

'Not far.' Gareth sounded impatient. 'Caroline, I *know* what Sandra said.'

'You—you do?' Caroline was taut.

'She deliberately omitted to tell you where David was.'

'What?' Caroline stared at him. 'But why?'

Gareth sighed. 'I imagine it was because we had had words—over you.'

Caroline bent her head. 'Was this before or after you asked her to marry you?'

The car ground to a halt. '*I* asked *her* to marry me?' he exclaimed. 'Who told you I did that?'

Caroline sighed. 'She did.'

'When?'

'Yesterday, as a matter of fact.'

'Oh, Caroline!' He pulled her to him urgently. 'And you believed her? Dear God, what a woman!'

Caroline couldn't resist the warm male strength of him. 'It seemed reasonable,' she whispered against his chest.

Gareth nodded. 'I imagine it would, then.' He stroked her cheek. 'Two days—no, three days ago, I told Sandra that you were the woman I had once been in love with——' He half smiled. '*Once*? God, I never stopped loving you!'

175

He paused. 'I told her because—well, because she was beginning to read too much into our relationship, hers and mine, and I had to make it plain that I had no intention of —well, making another disastrous mistake by marrying a woman I didn't love.'

'Oh, Gareth!'

'I thought she took it quite well. Maybe she thought I'd change my mind, I don't know. You see, I also told her that so far as you and I were concerned—well, that was long over.' He smoothed his thumbs against her temples. 'She must have discovered that we spent the day together at Nyshasa and decided to lie about our relationship in the hope that you'd never find out.'

Caroline drew back from him. 'And—and if this hadn't happened? My accident—oh, and Jeremy coming here— what would you have done? Would you have let me go back to England?'

Gareth tugged rather impatiently at the hair on the nape of his neck. 'Oh, God, I don't know. I doubt it. You must have noticed—I can't keep away from you no matter how I try.'

Caroline's brows drew together. 'That day at Nicolas's —and the other occasion you came when—when my arm was swollen——'

'Yes. That was some occasion, wasn't it?' Gareth's mouth was grim suddenly. 'That was one time when I had no defence against my feelings for you. And when you started taunting me ...' He shook his head. 'I could have —well——' He paused, and turned back to the steering wheel. 'We'd better go. We've got plenty of time to talk it all out.'

'Yes.' Caroline drew the rug closer about her. 'Did Sandra say why she—why she didn't tell me where David had gone?'

'She did eventually,' said Gareth shortly, putting the car into gear. 'Apparently she wanted to teach you a lesson. She thinks as a nanny for the children, you're singularly lacking in qualities.'

'Yes, I had gathered that.'

Caroline sounded taut and Gareth glanced at her again. Then he turned determinedly back to his driving. 'Caroline, I can't say everything I want to say now—not by any means. Let's just go back to the bungalow and talk later.'

'All right.'

Caroline nodded. She felt unaccountably chilled. In this mood he still had the power to reduce her to an incoherent schoolgirl, and he was deliberately creating a rift between them. Why? Was he already regretting his impulsive behaviour? Had he allowed his physical attraction towards her to outweigh his common sense? She had no way of knowing, but she longed for the formalities to be over and for them to have enough time to find out everything about one another.

Caroline awakened the next morning to find her room filled with light. The sun was already high and she sat up abruptly, wincing as her head reminded her of her accident the night before. But what time was it? She had not expected to sleep at all and now here she was, obviously oversleeping, and no one was coming to wake her.

She slid determinedly out of bed. There were so many things she had to do, and the realisation that soon she would see Gareth again filled her with excitement. It would be marvellous to be with him, to touch him, to share everything with him and know that he wanted to be with her.

As she washed in the usual brackish water in her bowl she thought rather reluctantly about Jeremy. She still had him to face. Last night in the upheaval of her return, in

177

Elizabeth's concern that she should have a shower and go straight to bed, she had not had any opportunity to do more than greet him, and she had sensed his annoyance at this state of affairs.

Drying her face on the towel, she felt a twinge of anxiety. She hoped Gareth returned this morning as he had said he would. He, too, had had no further opportunity of speaking with her, and after assuring himself that she was in good hands had left almost at once. She had not wanted him to go. She had tried to catch his eye, to intimate to him that of all people he should not leave her, but he had avoided her gaze and after a casual word with Charles had left for Nyshasa.

She sighed. The sooner she got dressed and spoke to Jeremy the better. She didn't honestly understand why he should have taken the trouble to come all this way to see her when she had told him distinctly that they were to be away six weeks. But perhaps a little of her pique at this was due to the fact that his presence had complicated matters.

She dressed with care in a tunic of apricot linen with side slits that revealed a length of slender tanned leg, and brushed her hair into loose order about her cheeks. Then she left her room and walked to the lounge.

She heard voices as she went along the passage and when she reached the lounge door she found Charles, Elizabeth, and Jeremy all sitting talking together.

'Caroline!' Jeremy sprang to his feet as soon as he saw her. 'Darling! How are you this morning? Oh, I've been waiting so impatiently for you to wake up. Do you realise it's almost half past ten?'

Caroline managed a smile. 'Hello, Jeremy.' Then she looked at the others. 'Good morning.'

Charles and Elizabeth both greeted her warmly, asking

178

how she was, Charles getting to his feet to examine the cut on her head.

'Oh, that's all right,' he assured her. 'You'll live!'

Caroline ran tentative fingers over the scar. 'I think I was very lucky. Where are the children?'

'Oh, they're out back,' replied Elizabeth, standing up too. 'You can see them later. They've been agitating to wake you up since just after nine. Now——' she glanced at her husband, 'you'd like some coffee?'

'I'd love some,' Charles nodded. 'I'll give you a hand.'

After they had gone, Jeremy smiled. 'That was very tactful, wasn't it?' he remarked. Then: 'Come and sit down. I want to look at you. I want to kiss you——'

'No, Jeremy,' Caroline interrupted him, going to sit on an easy chair. 'I—I don't want you to kiss me. I'm going to marry someone else.'

Jeremy looked taken aback. He didn't sit down, but stood staring at her as if he couldn't believe his ears. 'You can't be serious.'

'You know I am, Jeremy. I told you before I came out here that——'

'I know what you told me, Caroline. You mean to say you're seriously intending to marry this man—this Gareth Morgan?'

'That's right.'

'I suppose that's why he brought you back half naked last night!' snapped Jeremy angrily.

Caroline sighed. 'Jeremy, I know you're hurt and angry, but I did warn you. What are you doing out here anyway?'

Jeremy heaved a sigh. 'I came to tell you that my father died ten days ago.'

'Oh, Jeremy!' Caroline stood up, staring at him. 'Oh, Jeremy, I'm terribly sorry. Was it very sudden?'

'A coronary.' Jeremy thrust his hands into his trousers

pockets. 'You don't seem to realise what this means.'

Caroline frowned. 'Why, you'll be *Sir* Jeremy Brent now.'

'You think that's all?'

Caroline shrugged. 'I haven't thought about it.'

'Then perhaps you should. I'm going to have to give up teaching to go and take charge of my father's estate. I shall be the country squire. Doesn't the idea of being Lady Brent appeal to you?'

Caroline twisted her hands together. 'Oh, Jeremy, did you really think it would?'

He had the grace to look shamefaced. 'No—no, I suppose not. I—I hoped, of course.'

Caroline shook her head. 'Well, I'm awfully sorry about your father——'

'I'm sure you are.' Jeremy was stiff. Then he turned to her, his expression mirroring his frustration. 'Caroline, you can't really mean to tell me that you're going to stay here—in this godforsaken spot with—with that man?'

'If this is where he is, then this is where I shall be,' she replied simply.

'But—but you can't!'

'I'm afraid I can.'

When Charles and Elizabeth returned, the atmosphere was charged and even they could sense it. 'Well,' said Charles jovially, unaware of the tensions involved, 'wasn't it a lovely surprise for you finding Jeremy here when you got back last night, Caroline?'

Caroline bit her lip. 'Look, Charles, I think I ought to tell you—Jeremy and I are not engaged. We were. But not any longer. Nor is that situation likely to alter, do I make myself clear?'

Elizabeth looked astounded. 'And have you heard Jeremy's news?'

'About his father dying—yes,' Caroline nodded.

Elizabeth shook her head in a perplexed fashion and looked at her husband. 'I see,' she said.

'I'd like to make arrangements to return to England right away,' said Jeremy stiffly. 'Can I return to Ashenghi today?'

Charles exchanged glances with Caroline. 'I—er—I don't see why not.' He made a helpless gesture. 'Are you sure you don't want to stay on for a couple of days——'

His words hinted at some kind of reconciliation, but after looking at Caroline's set face Jeremy shook his head. 'No, thanks,' he asserted quietly. 'I'll leave this afternoon.'

The rest of the morning was quite an anti-climax. Caroline wandered about aimlessly, trying not to wonder what Gareth was doing, sharing a game with the children without really being involved.

Jeremy left soon after two. He bade Caroline goodbye rather pompously, she thought, and she guessed with a deep sense of sympathy that he was hiding his real feelings in this way. She watched the car until it was out of sight and then she went into the bungalow.

Elizabeth was stretched out on the couch when she entered and waved a languid hand. 'Has he gone?'

Caroline nodded. 'Elizabeth, have you seen Gareth about the settlement today?'

Elizabeth frowned. 'Not since he left here this morning.'

'This morning?' Caroline stared at her. 'He was here this morning?'

'Yes. Soon after nine. Long before you were up.'

Caroline's heart pounded. 'What happened?'

'He wanted to see you. Jeremy told him you were still sleeping and he went away again.'

'*Jeremy* told him?'

'That's right. He was in the lounge when Gareth called. I wasn't even dressed.'

'And what else was said?'

181

'How should I know?' Elizabeth stared at her. 'Does it matter?'

'It might.' Caroline turned back to her. 'Elizabeth, last night Gareth asked me to marry him.'

'What!' Elizabeth was astounded. She swung her legs to the floor and sat up. 'And—did you accept?'

Caroline nodded. 'Yes. Oh, yes, I accepted.'

Elizabeth narrowed her eyes. 'Why, you little——' She broke off, her face widening into a smile. 'I do believe that's why you agreed to come out here.'

Caroline flushed scarlet. 'I—I did want to see him again,' she admitted.

'Well, by gosh, doesn't that beat all!' Elizabeth was clearly too bemused to be angry. 'Wait until I see Gareth! I'll have something to say to him. We all thought he was interested in Sandra.'

'Yes. So did she,' said Caroline uneasily. 'Oh, Elizabeth, I'm worried!'

'Worried? Why?'

'Well, don't you see? Gareth said he would come back here this morning, and he did. But he saw Jeremy—Jeremy who still didn't know I wasn't going to marry him——'

'You mean you think Jeremy might have convinced Gareth that you were going to marry him after all?'

'It's possible. Oh, I don't know, Elizabeth. I just wish Gareth would come.'

But he didn't come, and the afternoon drew into early evening without any sign of him. Charles, who had visited the mine in the afternoon, returned home to find Caroline pacing the lounge dejectedly. It was Elizabeth who finally said:

'I suggest you take Caroline up to Nyshasa, Charles. Do you know where Gareth lives?'

'Of course I know,' Charles nodded.

'Then go ahead. Or this girl is going to have a fever sky-high!'

Caroline looked at Elizabeth. 'Wouldn't you mind?'

Elizabeth grimaced. 'Not so long as you send Charles straight back. I don't want him spending hours in the car waiting for you.'

Caroline managed a faint smile, but her nerves were as taut as violin strings. She was almost convinced that Jeremy had said something, but what if he hadn't? What if it was Gareth who had had second thoughts?

The drive to Nyshasa had never seemed so long or so arduous. The rains of the night before had left the roads thick with mud and slippery, and the station wagon's wheels skidded dangerously on corners. But at last the bridge over the falls was accomplished and Charles turned in the direction of the construction site. But long before they reached it, he turned off the road, through a belt of trees to where several bungalows faced a central courtyard.

'This is it!' he declared, pointing to one of the buildings where a light glowed. 'And that's Gareth's bungalow there. Do you want me to wait until you've spoken to him?'

Caroline scrambled out, shaking her head. 'No—no, Charles, you go. If—if you're not here he can't send me away, can he?'

Charles moved his shoulders. 'If you say not.'

'Thanks for bringing me.'

'You're welcome,' Charles nodded, and swung the vehicle round in a wide semi-circle before driving back through the belt of trees to the road.

After he had gone, Caroline stood still for a moment, summoning all her courage to go and knock at Gareth's door. What if he was not alone? What if Sandra was there? What would she do?

She half wished she had asked Charles to wait, but it was

too late now. She was committed, and she might as well go and get it over with.

A sudden roar erupted in the forest behind her and with a stifled scream she fled across the courtyard to Gareth's door, hammering on it with unnecessary force. But the unexpected sound had frightened her and she had visions of some predator stalking out of the jungle to carry her off.

There were footsteps beyond the door, and presently she heard the sound of the inner mesh door being opened, and then the outer door was pressed back, almost knocking her off her feet. Caroline stepped back, pale and slender in the moonlight, and stared at the man who was now profiled by the light from inside.

'Hello, Gareth,' she managed. 'Surprise, surprise!'

Gareth stared at her as if he couldn't believe his eyes. Then the roar came again, and she took a tentative step forward, glancing uneasily over her shoulder. 'Can I come in?'

Gareth hesitated only a moment and then he stepped silently aside for her to pass him into the hall. The outer door was closed and the mesh door swung into place, securing them in a lamplit world of warmth and comfort.

Caroline walked ahead of him into the living-room. It was a much more attractive room than the room at the Laceys' bungalow. The furniture was vinyl, there were coloured rugs on the floor, and the bookshelves flanking the empty fireplace were filled with books and magazines. The whole had a comfortable, lived-in air, and a delicious smell of coffee permeated from the kitchen.

Nerves controlling her movements, she swung round. 'What a nice room,' she said unevenly. 'Am I interrupting anything? Are you working?' She indicated some drawings laid out on the table in the dining area at the end.

'I was just checking something,' replied Gareth briefly.

184

'You haven't driven here alone, have you?'

'No. Charles brought me.'

'Then where is he?' Gareth frowned.

'He's gone back.' Caroline tried to speak casually, but failed abysmally, her voice breaking annoyingly. 'I—I thought you were coming to see me today.'

Gareth thrust his hands into the pockets of his close-fitting denim trousers. 'I did come, this morning,' he replied. 'But you weren't available.'

'I was asleep!'

'As I said, you weren't available.'

'Couldn't you have waited?'

'For what?' Gareth looked down at his stockinged feet. 'I spoke to—to Jeremy Brent.'

'And what did he tell you?'

'It's what he didn't tell me that's more to the point!' said Gareth shortly. 'I thought you were going to tell him you couldn't marry him?'

'I was—I did! This morning!' Caroline stared at him in consternation. 'Gareth, no one would let me speak to him last night.'

Gareth frowned. 'Did he tell you about his father dying and leaving him these estates—his title?'

'Oh, Gareth!' Caroline felt the hot tears brimming her eyes. 'You surely don't imagine that means anything to me!' She turned away, struggling to find a handkerchief. 'Oh, what an opinion you have of me!'

And then he moved, his arms closing round her from behind, dragging her roughly back against him, making her overwhelmingly aware of his urgent need of her. 'Oh, Caroline,' he groaned huskily, 'I'm sorry, I'm sorry. But I've been alone too long to accept paradise when it's offered to me. I feel there has to be a catch—that something will happen to take it away from me. Brent's news seemed to

185

me like that something. God, I wanted to tell him that you weren't marrying him—that I'd kill you before I'd let you go. But I couldn't. I couldn't force you to stay with me. It had to be your decision or not at all.' His hands caressed her passionately. 'All afternoon, I wondered what you were doing—I had visions of you going back to England with him and never seeing me again!'

'Oh, Gareth!' She twisted round in his arms so that she could see him. 'And I thought you'd had second thoughts—that you wanted Sandra after all.'

'Sandra?' His mouth sought hers hungrily. 'I don't want Sandra—I just want you!'

For a long while there was silence in the lamplit room and then Gareth drew himself reluctantly away from her. 'Do you want some coffee?' he asked, and she nodded, following him into the kitchen, unable to leave him alone.

'Will we live here?' she asked. 'When we're married?'

'Do you think you can bear to?' Gareth switched on the percolator and pulled her to him again.

'I really don't mind where we live,' she murmured honestly. 'So long as we're together.'

Gareth buried his face in her hair. 'Hmm, you smell good,' he murmured, unbuttoning the neckline of her dress to seek the creamy skin of her throat with his lips. 'However am I going to let you go?'

Caroline drew back to look at him, anxiety evident in her expression. 'To let me go?' she echoed. 'I don't understand——'

A rather satisfied smile touched the corners of his mouth. 'Oh, Caroline,' he breathed, against her ear, 'Laurie will marry us just as soon as I can make the necessary arrangements, but it won't be tonight, will it?'

Caroline quivered. 'Don't send me back to La Vache tonight,' she begged. 'The roads are slippery. I should hate

186

to think of you driving back here alone.'

Gareth studied her intently. 'What would you have me do?'

Caroline moved her shoulders in an eloquent gesture. 'Don't you have two bedrooms?'

'Three, actually—'

'There you are, then,' Caroline smiled. 'I'll stay here. If you'll have me.'

'You trust me to that extent?' Gareth watched her carefully. 'Aren't you afraid I might take advantage of you and then refuse to marry you?'

Caroline smiled then, a slow, assured smile. 'No. I'm not afraid. You see,' she added simply, 'the man I love wouldn't do a thing like that. He's an honourable man—that's why I love him.'

Gareth's eyes darkened passionately. 'All right, all right,' he muttered thickly, 'you can stay here. God knows I don't want to send you away. But I'm only human, Caroline, and it had better not be too many nights before we share a bed as well as a house!'

Caroline drew a trembling breath. 'I wonder what Nicolas will say when he finds out we're married.'

Gareth's palms rested against her neck, and there was an impatient look in his eyes now. 'Oh, yes,' he said. 'That's quite a thought.' His eyes narrowed. 'You did that deliberately, didn't you? Associating with him! Just to infuriate me!'

Caroline's lips twitched. 'I didn't—associate—with him. I was only alone with him once and then you came and broke it up. But I admit, I did—try to make you jealous.'

'You succeeded—admirably.' Gareth's hands tightened perceptibly. 'There were times when I——' He shook his head. 'Well, never mind. That won't happen again.' He touched his mouth to the corner of hers. 'I love you.' He pushed her firmly away from him. 'Now go away and let me pour this coffee before it begins to taste bitter.'

Caroline lingered by the door, watching him. 'I know someone who'll be pleased,' she murmured.

Gareth looked up. 'Oh, yes?'

'Yes. Helen.'

'Helen Barclay?' Gareth considered what she had said. 'Yes, I think perhaps you could be right. She was curiously abrupt with me when I was at the Mission yesterday.'

Caroline chuckled. 'Was she indeed?'

Gareth left the percolator to approach her perceptively. 'What do you know about it?' he demanded, reaching for her.

Caroline stepped back in mock-alarm. 'Only that I told Helen about—about us—a couple of days ago.'

Gareth caught her wrists, twisting them behind his back so that she was brought close against him. 'Did you really?' he murmured, looking down at her helpless predicament with a great deal of enjoyment. 'And what did she say?'

Caroline's eyes were on a level with the open neck of his shirt, and leaning forward she put her lips to the hair-roughened skin of his chest. 'Can't you guess?' she asked, against his flesh, and he released her wrists to put his arms round her.

'I gather she approved of you as an adequate wife for me,' he replied, his mouth warm and passionate against her shoulder.

Caroline nodded. 'That's right, she did.'

'Then that's all right, isn't it,' Gareth remarked, with a certain gentle mockery, 'because I approve of you, too ...'

Mills & Boon Classics

The very best of Mills & Boon
romances, brought back for those of you
who missed reading them when they
were first published.

There are three other Classics for you to collect this
November

SAVAGE LAND
by *Janet Dailey*

When Coley left the city for a cattle ranch in Texas she
was prepared to find certain changes in her way of life.
But she was to find that dealing with the brooding
Jason Savage was to bring her greater problems than
even she had anticipated ...

THE TOWER OF THE CAPTIVE
by *Violet Winspear*

Don Rafael had a Spanish attitude towards the amount
of freedom women should have, and Vanessa had an
Anglo-Saxon attitude. This was all right — until Vanessa
fell in love with Rafael.

PARISIAN ADVENTURE
by *Elizabeth Ashton*

It was perhaps because of Renée's resemblance to the
famous model, Antoinette, that she found herself
transported suddenly from London to the salons of Paris.
The famous couturier, Léon Sebastien, needed a replacement for Antoinette and Renée filled the bill. Rumour
also had it that Léon needed a replacement for
Antoinette in more ways than one!

Mills & Boon Classics

The very best of Mills & Boon
romances, brought back for those of you
who missed reading them when they
were first published.

In

December

we bring back the following four
great romantic titles.

THE BEADS OF NEMESIS
by Elizabeth Hunter

Pericles Holmes had married Morag Grant as a matter of
convenience, but she had lost no time in falling in love with
him. Whereupon her beautiful stepsister Delia, who always
got everything she wanted, announced that she wanted
Pericles!

HEART OF THE LION
by Roberta Leigh

When Philippa encouraged young Cathy Joyce to elope, she
didn't know the girl was the niece of her boss, the formidable
newspaper tycoon Marius Lyon — but that didn't stop him
promptly giving her the sack. But that was by no means the
last of Marius as far as Philippa was concerned!

THE IRON MAN
by Kay Thorpe

When Kim had no news of her fiancé in the Sierra Leone she
decided to go and find out what had happened to him. And
encountered opposition in the shape of the domineering
Dave Nelson who told her, 'Don't run away with the notion
that being female gives you any special immunity where I'm
concerned.'

THE RAINBOW BIRD
by Margaret Way

Paige Norton was visiting the vast Benedict cattle empire as
the guest of Joel Benedict. She had looked forward to it
immensely, although she hadn't much liked the sound of
Joel's stepbrother Ty, the boss of the station. And when she
met Ty, she liked the reality even less . . .

The Mills & Boon Rose is the Rose of Romance

Every month there are ten new titles to choose from — ten new stories about people falling in love, people you want to read about, people in exciting, far-away places. Choose Mills & Boon. It's your way of relaxing:

November's titles are:

IMAGES OF LOVE *by Anne Mather*
Tobie couldn't resist seeing Robert Lang again, to exact her revenge — but she didn't know what had happened to Robert since they had last met . . .

BRAND OF POSSESSION *by Carole Mortimer*
Jake Weston's lack of trust in her ought to have killed all the love Stacy felt for him — but it didn't.

DIFFICULT DECISION *by Janet Dailey*
Deborah knew that her job as secretary to the forceful Zane Wilding would be difficult — but the real challenge was to her emotions . . .

HANNAH *by Betty Neels*
Nurse Hannah Lang was happy to accompany the van Eysinks back to Holland, but the unbending Doctor Valentijn van Bertes was not quite so enthusiastic about it.

A SECRET AFFAIR *by Lilian Peake*
As a confidential secretary, Alicia was well aware how essential it was to keep secret about her boss's new project. So why didn't he trust her?

THE WILD MAN *by Margaret Rome*
Rebel soon realised how Luiz Manchete had earned his name — the wild man — when she found herself alone with him in the heart of his jungle kingdom . . .

STRANGER IN THE NIGHT *by Charlotte Lamb*
When Clare met Macey Janson, she began to lose some of her fear of men. So why did Luke Murry have to turn up again, making Macey suspect the worst of her?

RACE AGAINST LOVE *by Sally Wentworth*
Toni disliked Adam Yorke intensely, and her friend Carinna was more than welcome to him! But did Toni *really* mean that?

DECEPTION *by Margaret Pargeter*
Sick to death of being run after for her money, Thea ran away herself — but she only found a new set of problems . . .

FROZEN HEART *by Daphne Clair*
Joining an expedition to the Antarctic, Kerin was taken aback to discover that the arrogant Dain Ransome was to be its leader . . .